Secrets Of The Downpour

An Original Willow Academy Novel

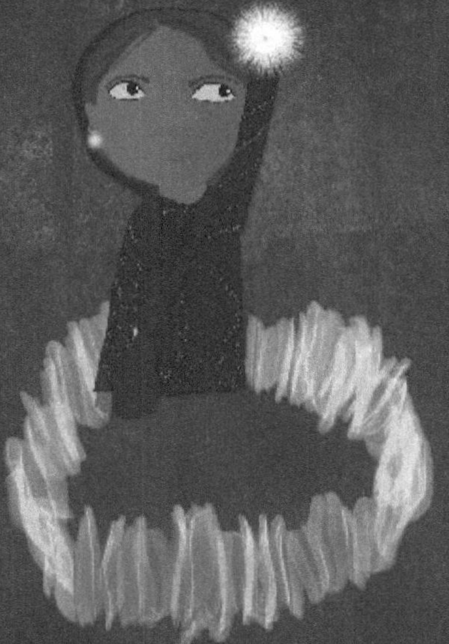

Pila Chapman

SECRETS OF THE DOWNPOUR

First edition. December 4, 2024.

ISBN: 979-8230951155

Written by Pila Chapman.

Table of Contents

I would like to dedicate this book to my family.
Especially to my little brother who would not read
this book until it was published and printed!

Special thanks to my writing teacher as well for
inspiring and encouraging me to write this book in the
first place!

Prologue:

"Now what do we do?" a woman asks. She is in a meeting with the other elders at Willow Academy, discussing the disappearance of the professor.

"You sure she is missing and not just on another adventure?" a man asks.

"Yes. Not even her apprentice knows where she is," the woman answers.

"Poor child. She is only nine. Erase her memory of her family and Obsidian so she is not grief-ridden. Leave Ateil though. She must remember her. Erase her memory of how to use her powers so Zara cannot track her. Most importantly, we must erase her memory of being the Guardian. Erase everyone's memory of her being the Guardian. The spells must wear off in exactly two years. We will ask Obsidian to watch over her. He will give her the riddle when the downpour has arrived," the worm queen says.

The man and woman look at each other. Obsidian is the most powerful Camishift. He is smart but a little wild to handle a child who is only a year younger than him. They must trust Acari though. It is not like they have a choice anyway.

"One more thing," the man says. "I think the Academy must be shut down. We must isolate everyone before Zara corrupts or kidnaps anyone else."

"Agreed," the woman and the worm queen say.

"What will we do with the child until then?" the woman asks.

The man turns to the worm queen. She had had a vision of this meeting. She knew what to do.

"Hide her. Somewhere deep in the Hidden Forest where she will not be found by Zara. And bring me Obsidian!" the worm queen orders a servant.

"This meeting is over. We must have faith in Lyra," the woman says. *"And in this crazy vision the queen had about this meeting and Obsidian,"* she adds in her mind. But she is respectful enough not to say that out loud.

Two years later...

Chapter One: My Generator Breaks And Nearly My Window Too

"Splutter, splutter!" is the sound my generator makes when I try to get it to work. I pull the cord again, but it is no use. I shiver as the cold rain trickles into my raincoat and down my back. This rain is nothing like the rain in Hawaii where you can run around in a dress in the rain and not be cold. This rain is the evil rain that makes you long for sunshine or a movie with hot chocolate and presents. This is the rain that cuts the power out and forces you to go outside to get the generator up and running. It is the same rain that is stopping me from sneaking over to the gas station to steal some gas for the generator, so it doesn't go splutter, splutter. It would be too dangerous.

This rain is just plain evil.

It just pours harder and harder the more you walk and stops when you go inside. I can't stop it, which is surprising. Though, I can't quite remember how I would stop it. There is magic at work here and I am going to find out why.

I head inside and dump my rain gear on the floor near the door.

I heat up some hot chocolate. You can't solve a puzzle without brain food! (This food warms up your brain. Literally.)

I turn the fireplace on to warm my shivering bones. Good thing this thing runs on propane otherwise I would have no heat.

Thunk! I hear on my skylight. Thunk! Thunk! I look up. Nothing but rain. Strange.

Thunk! Thunk! Thunk! On my window. Where have I heard that sound before?

Thunk! Thunk! Thunk! On my door. I slide over and open the door, but not too much though. Just enough so I can poke my head slightly out and call, "Who's there?" I haven't had a visitor in two years.

"About time!"

Chapter Two: The Least Sensible Day Ever

Without waiting for my invitation, a boy strolls in, dumping his jacket on the floor near the door with mine.

He has sharp, obsidian black hair, emerald-colored eyes, and loose-fitting rain pants with a navy blue sweatshirt.

"What do you think of this downpour Lyra?" Without waiting for my reply, he says, "This downpour is not natural. It's magical. I think someone is controlling the weather. Someone evil. Notice, how now that I am inside, the rain has stopped? It's almost as if this person doesn't want anyone outside because they're doing something unnatural. Now, have a seat."

Doing something? Interesting. Wait. Don't get distracted. This boy who I DO NOT KNOW literally walked right into my house, told *me* to have a seat, and told me my suspicions are right. I take a seat anyway and fiddle with my Nebula Moonstone earring. (Don't know what that is? It's because you are a Human.) I don't want to trust him, but I feel like I should because...

Oh! That's why the knock sounded familiar!

"You're Ateil's friend Obsidian!" I finally realize.

He frowns but seems to remember something and quickly hides it with a goofy grin. "At your service." He tips an imaginary hat and takes a seat in the other chair. "Now, you aren't causing the downpour which means that someone else is. Someone, who, like I said, is evil. Now, you need to find out who is causing this and why. This riddle will help you." He gets up and hands me a giant...*leaf*?

The riddle says:

> *This weather is evil magic,*
> *A magic very strong yet meek,*
> *Listen to the wind rustle and spin,*
> *Listen to the voices of the creek.*
> *This weather is evil magic,*
> *You have the power to halt it,*
> *Follow the words, the worm, the bird,*
> *And you will be able to stop it.*
> *This weather is evil magic,*
> *A magic you can not control,*
> *Try as they might, they won't win the fight,*
> *For you have a secret weapon to behold.*

"I'm sorry, what is *that* supposed to mea..." and he's gone. Probably should have seen that one coming. Okay. Looks like I'm on my own.

This should get interesting!

Chapter Three: The Whispering Winds

I am on a quest! This is going to be so fun and exciting! If only it wasn't raining. Lightning bolts.

I finally gather the nerve to brave the rain again. I shimmy into my rain pants, toss on my rain jacket, flip on my hood, and squeeze on my rain boots.

As soon as my foot leaves the door frame, it starts pouring again.

The Thump! Thump! Thump! Of the rain hitting my hood becomes a sound of evil.

The poem/riddle said to listen to the wind and then the creek.

I pull myself onto the lowest branch of Alaani, an oak tree in my yard. I close my eyes and strain to hear the wind.

Funny how when you try too hard to hear something, you can't hear it.

I'm trying to relax but I can't. My hands are so cold from the rain they feel numb. I tuck them into my pocket, but it doesn't help.

I sigh and open my eyes. This is not working.

A squirrel comes up to me. "*Chitter, chitter, chitter,*" he goes. "*Lean back, close your eyes, and listen,*" he says.

I take a deep breath. Close my eyes. Lean my head back. Listen.

I hear the birds fade into the background. The wind rustling the leaves. Spinning me into its secret language. A language only I can understand.

It's saying "*Zara, Zara, Zara,*" over and over again.

Where have I heard that name before?

My eyes fly open as I realize why the name sounds familiar.

"Ateil's arch nemesis!" I shout. I look around for confirmation. The squirrel gives me a tiny nod and scampers off.

Ateil and Zara were two weather sorceresses at Willow, the local school for the Magic People who understand Nature. A few animals go there too. Zara and Ateil used to be friends until... actually, I forget what happened between them. Soon, Zara disappeared as well as some Camishifts and other sorceresses. Then everyone disappeared.

I was Ateil's apprentice until she went missing two years ago. I was only nine. I've been living in my cabin deep in the Hidden Forest ever since. The Elders put me here, I think.

Last I remember, Zara wasn't strong enough to create a storm this big, much less hold one for this long. Then again, "last I remember" was two years ago.

But where is she hiding? In a desert, in a forest, at the bottom of the ocean?

Perhaps the creek knows the answer.

"Do you mind?" I ask Alaani.

Chapter Four: The Calling Of Clear Creek

She shoots out the branch I'm sitting on over the creek. Normally you would climb down the canyon wall to get to the creek, but the water is nearly to the top. This is dangerous. Now animals living on one side of the creek can't get to the other side. The creek is basically a raging river, though who it is raging at, I don't know. Zara perhaps?

I lean over and almost slip into the river.

"Woah!"

Branches quickly wrap around my ankles to keep me from falling in.

"Thank you. I know I nearly just fell to my death, but not so tight Alaani! You're cutting off my circulation," I reprimand.

Alaani responds by easing the pressure off my ankles.

Whoosh! Roar! Rumble! Is the sound of too much rain in the creek.

Usually, you will hear the faint trickle of water coming down the canyon wall. A gentle whoosh that almost sounds like a hum.

Stop. Focus! I need to know what the creek is telling me.

I lean back and close my eyes. Tuck my hands into my pockets. Listen.

The roaring of the creek blends into the sound of indistinct voices. I want to strain my ears to hear it, but I know better. I just relax and listen.

Soon the voices become clearer. Much clearer than any other creek I've listened to. That is why I call this creek Clear Creek.

I hear...

Zara and Ateil!

"It's been two years! Let me go!" Ateil shouts.

"When I finish my plan. You've been very helpful, allowing me to steal your powers against your will. The storms are a very good cover for what I am doing. No one dares to go out except for food, water, and their precious gas for their precious electricity. Now, back to where you belong!"

"But why did you bring me here to the redwoods? What is your plan? What are you going to do with Lyra?"

'Oh, don't worry about Lyra. As for my plan–"

Just like that the connection cut.

But it doesn't matter. I heard enough. Now I just have to do what the poem says. Follow the words.

Chapter Five: Words, Riddles, Poems, I Am Just About Done With All These Non-Straight Answers!

There are several... the best word I can find is *paths* in the Hidden Forest.

Each one leads to a different forest around the world. Some paths are easy to find like the bay paths and oak paths. Some are nearly impossible. Like the paths to the redwood forest.

I take out the leaf from my jacket pocket. "*Listen to the wind rustle and spin, listen to the voices of the creek.*" Check!

The next part though... "*Follow the words, the worms, the birds.*" That is what I have to do next.

I am following the words. To the redwood forest. But first, I need some supplies.

I run home and quickly toss two water bottles, some bars, cold tamales, an extra change of clothes, and a first aid kit into my waterproof satchel. I tuck a waterproof notebook into my pocket along with a pencil.

When I get outside, the downpour starts again, but it is different this time. The puddles are creating words!

I whip out my notebook and jot them down before the words disappear.

A magic word will win the worms over to your aide.

The magic word is a word of something that can grow, flicker and fade.

If you always do this, there is less of a chance for you to fail.

However, in this case, as long as you have this, you will prevail!

What am I?

"Um, what is that supposed to mean?!" I have just about had it with nonsensical answers and riddles. What can get you to win that can grow and flicker AND fade? Also, what can you do as well as have?

I sit down in the mud to think. SQUELCH! SQUISH! RUMBLE!

Wait, rumble? Oh no. A thunderstorm is coming! I have just about lost all hope of finding Ateil.

Wait. Hope. That's the answer to the riddle! Hope!

I am so excited about figuring out the magic word that I nearly forget that there is a thunderstorm. Until lightning hits the tree nearest to me and surrounds me with fire.

How the lightning surrounded me with all the mud I am not sure. Unless... unless Zara told it too.

Great. Now I am dealing with a ring of magic fire that wants to kidnap me.

Just great!

Chapter Six: The Magic Thunderstorm

Have you ever been surrounded by fire? Well, first things first, it is very hard to concentrate or think up a plan to escape.

How is the fire in the mud? I take a closer look. (Well, as close as I can get with fire.) I see that the fire is not burning on mud but rather really dry leaves. (How the leaves are dry with all the rain I have no idea. Unless Zara is behind the storm...)

Before I can finish that thought, Zara's voice booms loud and clear through the thunder. Yep. Guess she's behind the storm. "Lyra! Come and join me! I have your master with me as well. If you do not oblige, you will end up like her."

Well, both options sound absolutely awful. And I'm quite sure that Zara could hit me with a lightning bolt.

I can hear Zara's breath as a strong wind in the clouds as she waits for my answer.

I raise my hands above my head and try to summon more rain to put out the fire. No such luck.

She may not be able to see me (because then her face would make a cloud pattern in the storm), but she can certainly hear me. I need to escape as quietly as possible.

"What do you want me for?!" I shout as cover for all the noise I'm making.

I'm slowly lowering myself down and covering myself with mud. I reach down and grab two giant fists full of mud.

Zara keeps rambling on about how I can touch something she can't or something like that.

I quietly creep over to the ring of fire. (The one surrounding me, not the one in the ocean.)

Now for the most important part. I glance at the sky- Zara is still rambling on about something important but I'm too busy escaping to notice. I take a deep breath and toss the mud at the fire.

Hiss! Crackle! Pop! Is the sound the fire makes. I quickly rush through right before the flames engulf me.

I spot a cave in the ground and take cover in it. One last glance at the sky tells me Zara had her head too high in the clouds (quite literally) to notice my escape.

I snuggle closer into the ground. Now all there is to do is wait out the storm.

Chapter Seven: Finding A Frost Flower

After waiting half an hour, (I have a waterproof watch hidden under my sleeve), Zara still hasn't put out her fire.

My legs are starting to cramp. But as soon as I leave the cave, the fire will find me and the flames will try to trap me.

Unnoticed, unnoticed, unnoticed. That is the word I keep repeating in my head. The one thing saving me from getting fried to a crisp.

"Where to go, where to go?" I ask myself.

I snuggle closer into the mossy ground, resting my head on my satchel. I am stuck here with a fire out there and a giant gaping mouth of blackness behind me.

I need to find the worms. They will show me the way. Which way do I go? I need to escape! I finally decide on braving the gaping hole of blackness.

Except, once I go in, it is not black. It is a giant glistening cavern with Leprochite everywhere!

And there, standing on top of the podium, is a Frost Flower, in all its glory.

I had heard about Frost Flowers before. Whoever gets their hands on one has the power to create an ice age. If the wrong person gets their hands on it, something bad happens to them. I forget what though.

The Elders at Willow Academy had to hide or get rid of all the Frost Flowers for safety reasons.

I thought they were all gone. Turns out, I was wrong.

As I put my satchel on the ground (it was starting to get really heavy), I think about taking the Frost Flower. With this type of power, I could defeat Zara! Is it worth the risk though? The flower seems like it is practically calling out to me. Whispering my name. I can feel the power coming through its roots.

Then, without giving myself time to second guess my decision, I snatch it from the podium.

I reach into my pocket and find a scarf. (How did that get there?)

As I carefully wrap up the flower and tuck it into my satchel, I check my hands to make sure they are okay. They look fairly normal, so that's good! As I continue to examine myself, I spot a worm starting to tunnel into the cavern wall.

Finally! I'm getting out of here!

Chapter Eight: Following the Worms– No, Wait. Riding The Worm

Making sure the Frost Flower is secure in my pocket; I bend over and scoop up the worm. Gently cradling her in my hands, I whisper "Hope!"

Suddenly the worm leaps to life! (Quite literally!)

She leaps out of my hands and starts growing!

She grows larger and larger until she is the size of a jaguar!

"Hi there!" she says. "Thank you so much for freeing me from my curse. Is there any way I can repay you?"

I blink. Get a hold of yourself Lyra!

"Could you take me to the redwood forest?" I ask.

"Sure, hop on!"

Hop on? The poem didn't say anything about riding the worm. But seeing as I pretty much have no other choice, I snatch up my satchel and slowly climb onto her slimy back.

Not that much worse than the mud though.

"I'm Acari by the way."

"Lyra."

"Hang on! And close your mouth!" Acari gives the warning a little too late. She tunnels into the ground and I get a mouthful of mud.

Yuck!

We tunnel down and meet up with another tunnel. This one goes on and on forever! We have already traveled five miles.

All I have to do is listen to the *crunch*! *crunch*! of the still-dry leaves beneath Acari. A sound I never thought I would hear again.

Are we almost there? I want to ask. But that will have been the third time in the past five minutes. I know it has only been twenty minutes since I got onto Acari's back, but it feels like hours!

"Can you go *any* faster?" I complain, trying not to whine.

"Almost there," is her only reply.

"You said that three miles ago," I grumble.

I'm really hungry. As I search around my satchel for a snack, I ask, "Who put that curse on you?"

Acari sighs, sending a tremble through her body and nearly knocking me off.

"It was Zara's friend Camo. He's a Camishift– a shapeshifter. Plus a master trapper of the body or MTB for short. He can look like anyone and anything. He turned into a worm and tricked us all. For you see, we worms used to be the most powerful animals in the Hidden Forest. I was a queen, but then Camo came along a few years back and trapped us all so we could no longer think or talk. And he was oh so happy to gloat about how Zara had chosen him for the job. He kept going on and on about how he was the best Camishift in the world– oh look! We're here!"

Something that Acari said is nagging me at the back of my mind, but I shove it away. Oh– and forget the food. We have arrived.

Chapter Nine: The Marbled murrelet

The tunnel we were traveling through breaks through the ground and suddenly, I am in the heart of one of the last old-growth redwood forests.

Cool.

I slide off of Acari's back, making sure not to leave anything.

"Thank you for the ride, um, Your Majesty," I say, curtsying the best one can in a rain jacket and rain pants.

"You're welcome. I am off to recollect my subjects now that you have freed us. Take this amber. If you ever need us, squeeze it and it will alert us. Good luck!" With that, she flicks a piece of amber at me and tunnels down.

As I pick up the amber, I notice a worm stuck in it. Interesting. I tuck it into my raincoat pocket.

Now that I am not on a worm, I can finally eat. I find shelter in an old burned-out tree trunk and eat.

I do not notice the Marbled murrelet watching me with piercing eyes until he taps the tree trunk. *Thunk*! *Thunk*! *Thunk*! Almost the same way Obsidian tapped on my door...

Then I remember that I have to follow a bird to get to Zara.

Is this the right bird? Only one way to find out.

"Hello," I say in a soft voice to not scare the bird away. "I'm looking for someone named Zara. Can you help me find her?"

The bird goes Squark! Keer! Whistle! "Yes! Of course! Follow me!"

He takes off and I flip on my hood and chase after him, my boots sinking deeper into the mud with every step.

I chase after him for about six miles before he lands on a branch, a sign to take a break.

I sit down under a tree for shelter and drink some water.

"Want some?" I ask, offering the water in the direction of the marbled murrelet.

He nods.

"I'm not quite sure how to give this to you," I say, motioning towards his beak.

Then, a very strange thing happens. It is a phenomenon that I haven't seen in two years.

The bird flies down to the ground and turns into a boy! The bird is actually a Camishift!

He looks up at me with sparkling emerald-green eyes. "Can I still have that water?"

I star at him. Out of all the things I have seen today, this is by far the coolest and weirdest. I shake my head to clear it.

"Sure." I pull out my second water bottle and hand it to him.

I realize that I know this Camishift. It is Obsidian! The same boy who gave me the riddle.

"So, why were you a Marbled murrelet instead of just turning into a Magic Person? And also, if you knew where Zara was this whole entire time, why did you give me that confusing riddle?!" I try to keep my frustration from boiling over into my voice.

Chapter Ten: Finally, An Explanation!

Obsidian sighs and sits down. "I do suppose I owe you an explanation..." he begins.

"Well..." I prompt.

He sighs again. "Okay, I'll tell you. But you better sit down."

I sit down as he tells me to. But only because my legs are extremely tired and not because I am actually *following* his instructions.

"Okay. Long ago, the worm queen, Acari–I believe you met her– had a vision. You see, she was a visionary and a prophet. She could look into the future. But not just any future. The future that was the best for everyone. Then she would rewind and see how to get there. One da–"

That's as far as he gets before I interrupt him. "Wait, if she could see the future, why didn't she see Ateil getting kidnapped!"

"I must admit, I am not quite sure how that one slipped through her grasp. Anyway–"

"Why didn't she give me any information on how to stop her?"

"Maybe she did!" His voice was extremely patient considering how I keep interrupting him.

I open my mouth to ask another question.

"Stop asking questions and let me talk!" he exclaims.

So much for being patient. But I close my mouth and motion for him to continue.

"*Anyway*, one day, she had a vision of Zara stealing something important. Then a vision of her creating a downpour. A week into the downpour, she saw me giving you the riddle I gave you. Did you know that she had me watching over you for two years? She made me promise never to reveal myself before or after I gave you the riddle until it was time."

"How did you know when it was time?" I ask, unable to keep my mouth shut any longer. "And how did I never notice you?"

"Did you never notice me?" he asks, a sly smile on his face.

I think back. Then I realize, he sounds just like the squirrel I met earlier today. Wait, that was only this morning? Wow. I get lost in my head thinking about how many other times I've noticed him, oblivious to anything else. Until a large squabble pulls me back.

I pull myself back to the present.

"What was that?" I ask.

"I'm not sure." Obsidian tilts his head at me.

"What do you mean? That sound came from right in front of me!"

"You were lost in your head; I think your sense of direction was off because it was up in the trees."

Oh. Was he right?

Noticing me thinking about it, he smiles. "As for how I knew when it was time to reveal myself, I figured when you asked me if I was thirsty was a good time."

"Why didn't the worm queen just have you lead me to Zara if you already knew where she was? And how do you know where she is?"

"Acari told me. Also, Zara summoned me."

Oh. Right. I forgot that since people had such a hard time finding their Camishift kids, they started infusing them with a mineral or gem and naming them after it. Then, if you need to find them, you just squeeze the gem that is their namesake and they have no choice but to appear. That is what Zara must have done.

"Okay. Was that before you gave me the riddle?"

"No, right after. That is why I disappeared so suddenly."

Oh! I thought something seemed off about his exit! (Yes, I did, I can practically hear you laughing at me right now. Stop it!)

"I think Zara was trying to get me onto her side, but I refused. Also, I think maybe she wanted you to find something?" he hints.

I realize that he wants me to show him the Frost Flower.

"I didn't find anything," I lie, before I realize what I just did.

I'm not sure why I lied but something seemed off about Obsidian. He looked as if the second I showed him the Frost Flower, he would snatch it away from me.

A flicker of disappointment, anger, and... something else appears on his face, as if the only reason he came was to see the Frost Flower. He quickly covers it with a grin.

"Are you ready to defeat Zara because I sure am!" he exclaims.

Now that I am paying attention, it almost seems like he is reading these words off of a book or reciting a lie someone told him.

For a second, I wonder if he actually did agree to help Zara, but I quickly shove that thought away.

I had grown up with Obsidian for the first nine years of my life. He wouldn't betray me like that.

I realize he is still waiting for me to answer. "Okay. Let's go defeat Zara!"

Chapter Eleven: Has This Happened Before?

Obsidian stands up and dusts himself off.

"Ready?" he asks.

I nod.

"Great, let's go!" He gets ready to run, then seems to rethink his decision.

"On second thought, do you want a ride?"

"A ride?" I echo.

"Yeah, I can turn into a mountain lion, or a coyote, or a giant bird and you can ride on my back!" he explains.

"Well, I am pretty tired..."

"Great! Hop on!" He shifts into a mountain lion.

Before I know what I am doing, I swing one leg over his body, wrap my arms around his neck, and lean my cheek against his neck. This feels natural. But why? I don't remember ever riding Obsidian, or any Camishift for that matter. "Ready," I answer.

He shoots off like a rocket, bobbing and weaving through the trees as the rain pours down on our faces.

For some reason, this feels familiar. Like I have done this before. I try to remember why this feels so familiar. Like a dream that you can almost remember but not quite.

I try to shake off the thought that I have done this before. I have not. Or have I?

I sigh and try to relax into Obsidian's soft fur.

That also feels familiar. Why?

As we zig-zag through the forest, I close my eyes and feel the wind and rain against my face.

Then, I hear the strangest sound, a musical note that sounds like a sigh which almost sounds like it is pronouncing my name.

My eyes pop open. I scan the forest but don't see anything.

Obsidian doesn't slow down so he obviously doesn't hear it.

If he did hear it, he would have stopped and slowed down and begged me to go check out what it is with him.

How do I know that?

Obsidian growls. I realize I have been holding him too tight.

"Sorry," I whisper into his ear and relax my grip. I try to unsuccessfully stifle a yawn. I am SO tired!

"Why don't you rest for a little while? This is going to be a long ride!"

"I don't want... to... sleep..." Before I know it, I fall asleep, my head on top of his.

I dream about defeating Zara and finding my mother- my *mother?* I have a mother? Wait. What is a mo-ther? Sounds familiar. The dream changes. Now I am in a forest surrounded by thoughts and memories.

They all look familiar...

As I get close to remembering again, I slip off into a deep, dark, sleep.

Chapter Twelve: What The Weather Just Happened?!

I awaken as Obsidian starts to slow down. My first instinct is to sit up and stretch but then I hear a voice in my head. Obsidian's voice!

I had forgotten that he was one of the few rare people who could communicate using telepathy.

Wait. I am riding Obsidian, why is he talking telepathically to me? I relax and strain to hear his voice.

Suddenly, his voice comes through loud and clear. He says, *"Pretend to be asleep. Working on a plan. Zara won't hurt you. Don't wake up until I tell you too!"*

"Okay," I answer back.

Obsidian slows to a stop. I peek open an eye and my breath catches in my throat.

Right in front of me is Zara! What the weather is his plan?

"Good job *Obsidian*. Take her away. I will deal with her later."

"Yes, master."

What? I am so surprised that I cannot move and Obsidian moves quickly before I can get feeling back into my legs.

A ton of things happen very fast. Let me break them down for you:

1. I open my eyes and take a quick look around before Obsidian roughly drops me onto the ground.
2. I manage to see a giant camping tent and a small building, and that is all I see before:
3. He changes into a Magic Person and blindfolds me.
4. I am blindly led to somewhere. My feet keep stumbling on the uneven ground.
5. I am shoved into something. No, not shoved. More like, spun maybe? I don't know. It leaves a twisted sensation in my stomach. Where am I now? A cage perhaps or a dark room?
6. Obsidian pulls the blindfold off and melts into the shadows.

All this happens in about the span of two minutes.

Now it is just me.

I look around and see that I am in a *very* dark room with two single-lit candles and a couple of books for kids that are around the age of three. A few cockroaches are scuttling around too.

I sigh and lay down using my satchel as a pillow. I can't believe he didn't take it away from me.

I think back to what just happened.

My childhood friend Obsidian just turned me into *Zara* of all people. The person who stole my family!

Wait. How do I know that? Or am I just remembering?

Tears trickle down my face and I furiously wipe them away. I don't have time to cry!

I pushed myself up.

"WHAT THE WEATHER JUST HAPPENED?!" I yell.

"You were obviously just kidnapped," a voice deadpans, stating the obvious.

Chapter Thirteen: (The Real) Obsidian's Story

I freeze. Apparently, I am not the only person who Zara put into this dungeon thing.

"Who's there!" I ask, trying to keep my voice from shaking.

"What do you mean who's there? You know who!" the voice yells back.

I scan the dark room and there, in the corner, I spot a figure huddled against the wall. Obsidian!

"Why did you turn me in!" I yell, the fure in my voice bouncing off of the walls.

"What do you mean 'turned you in'?! You're the one who kidnapped me."

What? This conversation is obviously going nowhere fast.

I take a deep breath to calm myself. Obsidian was always rushing off to some adventure and usually, I could reason with him to keep him safe. (Why do I keep remembering things like this? Or more importantly, how did I forget that Obsidian is my best friend? Or what a mother is?)

"Obsidian," I say, trying to keep my voice level, "I don't know what happened. All I remember is that I was riding on your back and then you brought me he-" I cut off, remembering something Acari told me.

It was Zara's friend Camo. He's a Camishift– a shapeshifter. Plus a master trapper of the body or MTB for short. He can look like anyone and anything. He turned into a worm and tricked us all.

"It wasn't you," I say, realizing the truth. "It was Camo. He tricked me by turning into you and getting me to trust him because I thought he was you! He tricked you the same way, didn't he Obsidian?"

A beat of silence. "Is it really you this time?" he asks.

I nod then remember that he can't see me. "Yes. Search my memory if it helps."

Another beat of silence. Then- "It really is you!"

He launches himself at me and hugs me.

I laugh and wrap my arms around him, hugging him back tightly. It feels so good to be with the *real* Obsidian again.

"Can you tell me what happened?" I ask, pulling back.

Obsidian's expression darkens. "Well, I gave you the riddle. Then Zara summoned me. I think she knocked me out cold and put a tracker on me. Then I woke up in the forest, saw you, and turned into the squirrel that helped you and then flew off to the forest to be the marbled murrelet you saw. I didn't know they were tracking me. While you were lost in your head, Camo attacked me, and then Zara summoned me. Tossed me into here. She tried turning into you to get me to talk. The first time she played the trick, I fell for it. I listened to her thoughts when she first arrived. I told Zara that her thoughts sounded different than yours and then the connection cut. She must have turned on some mindblocker. I didn't think about how weird that was. Maybe if I had, you wouldn't be here." He looks at the ground and clears his throat.

I give him a small smile and squeeze on the arm to let him know that it was okay. "I would have fallen for it too."

He sniffles and gives me a small smile back before continuing his story. "I told Zara, who I thought was you, that Acari wanted you to geta Frost Flower and asked if you had it. That was when she revealed herself. I don't think she meant to. She said something about how she was getting Camishift lessons from Camo and she still hadn't mastered them yet."

"Zara knows I have a Frost Flower?"

"Sorry. I thought she was you."

"That's okay," I reassure him. NOT okay! But it is what it is and now we have to deal with it. I shiver and realize my rainpants and raincoat are soaking on the inside. Rain must have slipped in when I fell asleep on Obsi- I mean Camo. I slip off my pants and coat. "At least it is dry in here? Do you know how to escape?"

Obsidian shakes his head.

"Zara thought of everything. She created this room just for prisoners- specifically us. So I can't shift and you can't use your weather sorcery. I can't even use my telepathy!"

"How did you contact me then? Or was that Camo?"

"No, that was me. Zara pulled me out to show me you getting caught. That was when I contacted you. I knew it was risky considering you could be Camo, but I was desperate."

"That was the right choice," I assure him. "Can we escape through the door?"

"There are no doors"

"What about when she brings food?" I ask.

"All food gets Ttufosed in."

(Ttufos stands for Transportation Through the Universal Fabric Of Space.) Camo must have Ttufosed me in. That is why my stomach felt so twisty!

"Can we Ttufos out?"

"Sure, if you have been taking Self Ttufosing lessons!" he quips.

Self Ttufosing is Ttufosing without a Ttufos machine.

I frown. I don't remember Obsidian being so negative.

He must see my frown. "Sorry. I just really want to get out of here and I am really regretting not signing up for Self Ttufosing lessons right now."

"Me too. Remind me why we didn't sign up?"

"Because we never expected to be in an actual life version of the adventures we would make up when we were young. Remember the book series *Shammy Stories*? I would be Dimo and you would be Pila. I never dreamed we would be on a quest as cool as one of theirs!" he grins.

That's the Obsidian I remember!

I grin back. It is so good to have my best friend back!

Just then, there was a loud POP!

Me and Obsidian startle and jump up.

Standing in the middle of the room is a girl who looks about the age of nineteen. She looks nearly exactly like Zara except her hair is a light navy blue instead of Zara's fiery red and her eyes are much softer and kinder, and an aquamarine color compared to Zara's hard jade green.

Obsidian steps in front of me protectively. "Go away Zara!" he shouts.

The girl looks confused. "How do you know my name...
oh! You must be talking about my twin sister Zara! My name is
Xara. With an X!"

Me and Obsidian look at each other. *What the weather?*

Chapter Fourteen: These Identical Twins Are Nothing Like Each Other!

"Wait, Zara has a twin sister?" I ask. Judging by the look on Obsidian's face, he didn't know this either. The girl nods.

"Hold on. How do we know that you didn't just turn into a twin sister version of yourself?" Obsidian asks.

"He has a point."

The girl- Xara- sighs and looks hurt. "I guess there is no way that I can get you to trust me unless- oh!" Xara brightens and pulls out a device from her raincoat.

Obsidian and I instinctively step back.

"Don't worry. I can't hurt you with this," she says.

"What is that?" I narrow my eyes suspiciously.

Xara sighs again. "I suppose you really do have no reason to trust me considering that it was my sister that trapped you here." She taps a few buttons and suddenly, the room is illuminated as the lights flicker to life!

"Thank you?" Obsidian says, posing it as a question.

"No problem. I actually had a lot of fun sneaking about my sister's camp stealing stuff!"

Me and Obsidian glance at each other. Did she *actually* do that, or is that a lie?

"I can see you still don't trust me. How about this: I lower the brain blockers and you can search my brain for any bad intentions. Then, when you realize you can trust me, we all escape!"

Sounds easy enough... But...

"What's the catch?" I ask.

Xara smiles mischievously. "You let me help you take down my sister. So, what do you say?"

"Um..." I'm thinking... I'm thinking... still thinking...

Obsidian jumps in and does the thinking for us. "Deal!" he says and shakes her hand.

She smiles. "Fantastic. Also, how about we call my sister by her middle name, so we don't mix up me and my sister. Plus, she doesn't even like her middle name!"

"Okay, what is Zara's middle name?"

"Araz."

I laugh. "Isn't that just 'Zara' spelled backward?"

Xara laughs too. "It is! That is why she doesn't like it!"

"Okay!" Obsidian laughs. "Araz it is then! So, can you lower the brain blockade or whatever it is called?"

"Oh! Sure!" Xara pushes a button on the controller.

Obsidian closes his eyes and after five seconds, smiles.

"Well?" I ask.

"She's good!" he declares.

"Really? You were in her mind for about five seconds!"

"Only five? It felt like an hour! I thought you were going to give me a lecture on not wasting precious time."

"Hmph! Well, if an hour was five seconds, then go back for another five seconds and double-check. She may be able to hide her thoughts or intentions."

"Actually, I may be great at keeping secrets, but they literally bounce around my head all day. They are literally all I think about!"

"It's true," Obsidian confirms.

"Alright then. We should escape soon then. But first, are there recording devices or cameras in here?"

"Nope. I hacked every single one of my sister's computers and could not find any security cameras."

"Great. Because we are going to need a plan and the forest could be full of spies."

"Good thinking Lyra! We can hatch a plan in here where no one can hear us. Just one thing though," Obsidian says.

"What's that?" I ask.

"It's something that I should have told you the second I realized you were you."

"What's that?"

"At least a quarter of your memories are missing," he says.

What?

"What?!" I shout.

Chapter Fifteen: Escape!

Obsidian winces.

"Sorry," I mutter, rubbing my temples. This information is giving me a headache. "But seriously, what do you mean that *at least* a quarter of my memory is missing? And where? Who took my memory?"

Obsidian sighs and closes his eyes. "I did," he whispers. "I made you forget your family and how to use your magic. I'm sorry. I'm really, really, sorry."

I stare at him. Did he really just say that he took my memory away? I open my mouth to ask him why, but he beats me to my own question.

"Please don't be mad. I had to. Acari told me to or else Zara- I mean Araz would have found you ages ago."

The problem with this statement was that it was frustratingly true. Anyone could track a weather sorceress just based on their magic, unlike with Camishifts.

When I don't say anything, Obsidian hesitantly asks, "So, is that a mad silence, or a thinking silence? Or an 'I can't believe you never told me this before and I never want to talk to you again but I suppose I have no choice because I am going to need you to tell me where my memories are so I can defeat Araz' silence?"

I can't help myself; I smile. Obsidian has a way of doing that for you. "A combination of the first and last option I think."

He smiles.

A sudden BLEEP! BLEEP! BLEEP!!! comes from Xara's pocket.

"Do I want to know what that means?" I ask.

Xara shakes her head. "I bugged my sister and Camo and altered my phone to let me know when they are getting ready to Ttufos to my coordinates."

I gasp. "Quick! Obsidian, where are my memories hidden?"

"In Recollection Rainforest."

"Where all lost memories are hidden," Xara adds.

Oh. Am I the only one who doesn't know a thing about the Recollection Rainforest? Hmm. Why- stop! That's not important right now! "Great, let's go get my memories and then defeat Araz."

"I don't approve of that plan!" A voice comes from behind us. A voice we know.

We all freeze and turn around very slowly, as if that would change who is suddenly in the room with us.

"Ah! I see you have met my *sister*." Araz draws the word out like a sneer.

"Hello dear twin, I see you have dyed your hair again. Must I say that the red really disagrees with the jade-green color of your eyes," Xara says.

I stare at her. Is she *seriously* giving her sister *fashion* advice right now? Then I notice her hand. Even upside down, I can tell what she is signing: *Slowly walk towards me. If Araz notices, run!*

I get the message and start to creep towards her as she argues with Araz about the color of her coat. (Not a raincoat if you were wondering, it was a normal one as the rain seems to "ignore" her. *Annoying*!)

Unfortunately, Obsidian must not see Xara signing because he is currently slowly creeping *away* from Araz.

She notices him though, and quick as her lighting spins around and grabs him by the collar of his shirt.

"*Help!*" Obsidian's voice appears in my head.

Xara, however, is way ahead of me and tackles her sister from behind.

"Hey!" Araz shouts, tossing her hands up. This gives Obsidian the chance he needs to escape.

I rush over to him, pull him to his feet, and run over to help Xara with Obsidian hot on my heels.

"Xara!" I yell. "We need to go!"

She either ignores me or can't hear. I can't tell which. Both are highly probable because right now she is wrestling with her sister for the Ttufos machine!

"We have to help her!" Obsidian says.

I nod. Somehow, I know what to do. A new or old memory comes back to me of Obsidian and I in training. I think self-defense class, perhaps?

Obsidian and I are ran in perfect sync. He distracted while I tackled from behind, pelting them with hail. I don't remember who we were practicing on though.

While I blinded them with rain, Obsidian tied them up.

My body knows what to do. We move in perfect sync. Even more perfect than the sync we moved in in the memory. Obsidian yells at Araz, I tackle her back.

"Get off of me!" she screeches.

I look around for something to help me.

"Lyra, catch!" Obsidian tosses me my raincoat.

"*Tie. Her. Up!*"

I reach into my pocket and quickly pull out Acari's gift, then tie the sleeves around her neck, the hood momentarily blinding her.

"Let's go!" Xara shouts.

Obsidian and I rush over to her.

"Finally!" I say.

Xara punches in some coordinates while Obsidian and I cling onto her arm, and I feel the somewhat familiar sensation of Ttufosing.

Time and space wrap around me, my atoms nearly separating.

That soon ends and I crash onto the ground and Obsidian lands on top of me.

"Get off!" I say, my voice muffled in the moist dirt. He says nothing and I take that as a cue to shove him off of me.

He groans. "Where are we?"

"Recollection Rainforest," Xara says, sitting next to us on the muddy floor.

Chapter Sixteen: Recollection Rainforest

I sit up and look around. The first thing I notice is that it is not raining. We are surrounded by trees that are covered with white glowing orbs.

Beside me, Obsidian groans again.

"Are you okay?" I ask.

"Not really." He pulls up his pants leg and I gasp. His ankle is all red and swollen!

"You're hurt!" I cry, digging through my satchel for the first aid kit.

"Yep."

I finally find the first aid kit, but I have no idea what to do.

"Um, what do I do?"

"Here, let me," Xara offers.

Obsidian and I look at each other. Well, she just saved us, so I guess we can trust her.

Obsidian nods and I step aside as Xara pulls out a roll and stick and a weird-looking plastic package. She wraps the roll around the stick and plastic and ties it off.

"How's that?" she asks.

I offer him my hand as he shakily stands up.

"Good, thanks."

Xara nods and looks around. "There are hundreds of thousands of memories here! How will we find yours in time to stop Araz?"

"Um, what is Araz's plan anyway?" I ask.

"I... um... I think it would be better for you to find out for yourself," Xara says, not meeting my eyes.

"Lyra," Obsidian says suddenly, making me jump. I'd forgotten he was here, despite him leaning on my arm for support. "What is your favorite tree in the world?"

"You mean like, my favorite type of tree?"

"No, your favorite tree."

"Hmm." That's a hard one. My favorite tree. How could I ever choose just one?

"I think I would have to go with Alaani," I say. "Remember when we would climb her branches and pretend we were Dimo and Pila finding the Leprochite?"

"And how we would camp out in her branches and hide in her hole during hide and seek or when there was a thunderstorm?" Obsidian adds.

"Um, if you guys are done reminiscing, which tree is Alaani?" Xara interrupts.

"Hmm. She is an oak tree, about eleven years old. She looks like she has a face on her because of her bark pattern and her roots are slightly uprooted and twisted into a heart shape."

"Okay, everyone split up and search!" Xara exclaims.

"Is it safe?" I ask.

"Oh yes," Obsidian and Xara reply at the same time. They look at each other, surprised.

I guess I really am the only one who doesn't know a thing about the Recollection Rainforest.

"Okay," I say, my voice slightly shaky.

Obsidian must notice the tremble in my voice because he says, "Actually, since this is your first time here, why don't I go with you?"

I smile. "Sure."

"Great. You guys go left, I'll go right. Just holler if you find anything!" Xara says, already running off in the other direction.

She is soon out of sight and we start heading in the opposite direction of her fading figure.

"You didn't have to do that, you know," I tell Obsidian.

"I know, but I haven't gotten to spend time with my best friend in two years!"

I laugh. "I missed you too. Once I remembered you." I frown. "So, just what memories did you steal from me?"

"I didn't steal them!" Obsidian protests.

"Well, you didn't exactly ask me."

He laughs. "True. Let's see. Acari made me erase your memories of me, your mom, your dad, and your younger brother. As well as how to use your weather sorcery."

"I have a little brother?"

He nods.

Wow. I can't believe I forgot him.

"What happened?" I ask quietly.

"They were captured by Araz," he whispers, as if saying her name would summon her.

I ball my hands into a fist. All the more reason to find my memories and defeat Araz.

"Do any of these trees look like Alaani to you?" I ask.

Obsidian starts to say something but is cut off by Xara yelling, "Hey! Let go of me!"

"Looks like Xara found trouble!" Obsidian flashes me a grin and shifts into a black panther. "*Hop on!*" he says to my mind.

I grin and climb on, swinging my leg over his body, my arms wrapping around his neck, my cheek resting on the side of his neck. Just like how I did when I thought Camo was Obsidian. This time, it is with the real Obsidian.

"Let's go help Xara!" I say, and we take off.

Chapter Seventeen: My Memories

We rush through the forest, words calling out to me. I realize that when I was riding Camo, we must have neared the path to the Recollection Rainforest and those were the voices I had been hearing.

Obsidian skids to a stop, sending me flying off of his back.

"Hey!" I yell, though I'm not actually mad at him.

"Look Lyra! We found Alaani!"

I turn around. Obsidian was right. We did find Alaani. Swinging Xara back and forth by her ankle.

"Let go of me you, you, um... oak tree!"

Alaani responds by tossing her up in the air and catching her by her bright blue braid right before her feet hit the ground.

Xara groans, looks up, and catches sight of us.

"Hi. As I am sure you noticed, I found your tree, but she keeps grabbing me! I was going to be super dramatic and blow a conch shell or horn or something like that to tell you that I found her but then, well, this happened."

By "this", Alaani's new way of playing with her for the moment was cradling her like a baby and then tossing her in the air.

I can't help myself; I giggle. Which gets Obsidian laughing which gets me laughing until we are laughing so hard that we must lean on each other for support.

"Stop laughing!" Xara screeches, but she is laughing now too.

"Okay, okay! Pull it together!" I shout at myself. Then I reach out to Alaani. She immediately drops Xara on the ground and scoops me up.

I laugh. "Miss me much?" I stroke her rough cracked bark, thinking of how she used to hold me like this when I was little and got scared.

It was so- stop getting lost in the past Lyra! Okay. Focus! The task at hand.

"Can you show me the memories taken from me?"

Alaani glows bright violet and in a flash of light, everything disappears. For a second. Then, I am flooded with so many memories at once that I think my head is going to explode!

My mother. Her name is Aya. She is a Water Weaver. She is really smart and taught me about every single different kind of weather.

My father, Telek. He is a gravitational wizard. He taught me how to be a telepath. Wait- I am a telepath? Cool!

My little brother. James. He is a Camishift. He taught me how to have fun when I got older. Showed me his secret hiding spot with his baby animal friends.

I remember my aunt who is also my teacher. Her name is Islana. She is an Infuser.

I was the top student at school. I suddenly remember how to create a hailstorm and a thunderstorm. How to make the sun break through the clouds during a dark and scary storm. How to turn a cloud into a certain shape.

Most importantly, I remember something someone told me a long time ago. Their voice sounds like soothing waves in my ear as I listen to them whisper to me as a baby, *"You wield amazing power. You will be the most powerful Weather Sorceress ever. But someday you must make a choice that will decide the future of everyone. I draw power from the icy moons of our solar system, of the blizzards of the past, of the snow of today, and I give it all to you. One day, you will wield the last Frost Flower we have ever known. And you will defeat a great evil with it. Do not let its power consume you like its previous master. You are the Frost Flowers' new Guardian. Good luck, little moonstone."*

Moonstone. The name my family used to call me because of my moonstone-colored eyes.

Then I am falling, a long, long way down.

I wake up, five minutes or hours later. I can't tell. My head is resting on my satchel and Obsidian is pacing nervously in front of me while Xara is treating a cut on my arm.

I groan and sit up.

Xara helps me. Obsidian rushes over to my side.

"What happened? Did you get your memories back?"

I nod because my throat is so dry I can't speak.

He sits back, relieved. "Well, what did you remember? Anything on how to defeat Araz? Is your head okay? Does it feel like it is going to explode?"

"It will if you keep asking her questions!" Xara snaps.

That gets Obsidian to be quiet. "Sorry. I was just really worried."

"It's fine. Although my brain does feel like it might explode."

"Can you stand up?" Xara asks gently.

"I can try." I stand up and sway a little before Obsidian grabs my arm and stabilizes me.

"What did you remember?" he asks again.

I have read enough books to know that nothing good comes from not telling your friends what you remember, so I tell them everything. From remembering my family's names to the soothing wave voice that spoke to me telling me that I am the Guardian.

When I finish, they sit down, stunned.

"Um, hello? Did I just break your mind? I'm pretty sure I'm the only one around here who had a broken mind and now it is fixed."

Silence.

"Hello?!"

Obsidian laughs suddenly. "Lyra, that is the craziest, most wild story I have ever heard and if I heard it from someone else, I never would have believed it!"

I laugh.

"Wow. That is amazing! Is it true that you have a Frost Flower?" Xara asks. "I saw something about that in my sister's notes."

Obsidian winces.

I nod.

"Cool! Now that means that you are its Guardian. If anyone else touched it, they would have been frozen to the bone."

"I did not remember that when I grabbed it."

"This should be an adventure!" Obsidian smiles.

"Now that you have your memories back, should we come up with a plan to stop my sister?" Xara asks.

"Yeah!" Obsidian punches the air. "Let's go stop our friend's evil sister!"

Xara and I laugh at his choice of wording.

"Wait- we're friends?" she asks.

"Well, you did just rescue us, heal Obsidian's ankle, and my arm, so yeah. We're friends!" I tell her.

She smiles. "Great. Now, we are going to need a *really* good plan to defeat my sister."

"Hey Lyra, why don't you show us what you can do now," Obsidian says.

"Yes! Show us!" Xara exclaims.

"Show us! Show us! Show us!" they start to chant.

"Alright, alright! I'll show you. Just stop chanting! You're making me laugh so hard I can't concentrate!"

"Sorry!" They both shut their mouths and then burst out laughing.

I join them.

"Okay, okay, stop!" Obsidian shouts/laughs.

Xara and I finally get a hold of ourselves.

"Okay. Let's see what I can do!"

Chapter Eighteen: Practice Makes Perfect!

Wait, No. I Am Already Perfect!

I whip my hands around in a complicated motion and raise them to the sky. Suddenly, rain starts pouring down on us.

"Hey! Think you can stop the downpour? I think that I have seen enough rain in my life to last twenty years!" Obsidian grumbles as thunder rumbles overhead.

I slowly bring my hands down and the storm dissipates.

Before they know what hits them, I quickly whip my hands at Obsidian and Xara and send a tiny tornado their way.

"Woah! Put us down!" Xara yells.

I giggle and snap my fingers. The tornado disappears and drops my friends on the ground.

"Seriously?!" Xara exclaims.

"What?" I say, making my eyes wide and innocent. "You said to put you down."

"*Put* down, not *drop* down!"

I shrug and Xara pinches the bridge of her nose and sighs.

"Hey Lyra, can you still summon hail and drop it down on our head?" Obsidian asks.

"I can certainly try!" Reacting on instinct, I spin my hands, weaving a cloud, and fling it over at my friends. The cloud flies over and starts to pour golf ball-sized hail on them.

"Ahh! I take it back! I take it back! Stop before you leave golf ball-sized dents in our heads!" Obsidian hides under a tree root while Xara runs in a square pattern to try to escape my hailstorm.

"Oh, fine!" I pout. But I snap my fingers and the hailstorm stops pelting my friends.

"So, now we know that you can defend yourself with your weather. But what about if Araz takes away your power?" Obsidian asks.

"She can do that?"

"Between you and my sister, I am learning that anything is possible!" Xara says, making me smile.

"It wouldn't be smart though, because then she would have no control over the weather either," I point out.

"Hmm, you do make a good point," Xara admits. "But I've learned the hard way not to underestimate my sister."

"Okay. How about we come up with some, what's the word I'm looking for? Battle routines? We'll go with that word. Let's come up with some battle routines that we can use to defend ourselves," I say, thinking back to the self-defense classes we were required to take at Willow.

Obsidian must be thinking the same thing because he says, "Just like the self-defense classes we used to take!"

I laugh. "My thoughts exactly."

"Hey forest! Think you can turn into a copy of Araz's camp?" Xara asks.

The trees shudder in response. Suddenly, the forest melts away to reveal an exact copy of Araz's camp.

"Woah," is all I can say. "This is not real, right? We won't get captured?"

Xara laughs, but not in a mean way. More in a kind that 's-what-I-used-to-think way. "No. This is just a solid illusion. Hey, look! It even included a mini Araz and Camo to avoid. Now, let's train!"

We have fun climbing trees and running on rooftops as quietly as we can.

I relearn how to use my telepathy to communicate with Xara and Obsidian as we come up with a plan.

When anyone comes near us, we hide in the shadows. When they get farther away, we creep after them, silently. We are like a pack of coyotes. Hunting together. Staying safe together.

I spy on Araz and watch her crouch down to a tiny hole at the base of an odd redwood tree. I can't quite tell why it looks odd though. The hole is so tiny you would never notice it was there.

As I creep over to Illusion Araz, something catches my eye. I peek around a rhododendron bush and gasp.

There, on the other side of the bush are a bunch of stone figures. And the worst part of all, I recognize every single one of them.

The number of Magic People still alive is few. Too few. So few that you knew practically everyone in the village. And nearly everyone I used to know is here. Turned to stone.

Chapter Nineteen: Araz's Plan

"*Get over to the rhododendron bush now!*" I call in my mind.

Obsidian and Xara rush over five minutes later. By the time they get here, I have found my family. I give each of my stone-turned family members a hug and turn to Xara.

"What happened?" I ask, my voice shaky.

Obsidian rushes to my side and envelops me in a hug.

"*Thanks,*" I tell him with my mind.

Xara bites her lip. "This was my sister's doing. She drained every one of their magic and took it for herself. Without their magic, they couldn't survive so they turned into stone. Araz is planning on using that magic to hold up this storm while she searches for the two most magical objects in the universe."

"What are those?" I ask.

"The drop of solid light that keeps the Sun lit and the magic of Mother Nature. She is planning on stealing those for herself and becoming the most powerful person ever. Then, she will rule this galaxy and beyond with that power. She has already collected the solid drop of light that resides at the center of the Sun though I have no idea how she got it. That is another reason for the storm. Without the solid drop of light, the Sun can't stay lit for more than a few days and no one will notice that the Sun is not lit if they won't even go outside.

Without sunlight, the world will be cold. No one will notice that either since everyone is inside. Notice how it is freezing though?"

It is? Oh yeah! Now that I think about it, I am freezing!

I shiver and put on my extra jacket that was in my satchel.

"I'd say we have about five more days at the most before the Sun goes out. Indefinitely. Lyra, Araz needs *you* to collect the magic of Nature. Even with all the extra magic she stole, she cannot collect it without getting incinerated. Only someone with an insane amount of magic and trustworthiness can collect it without, to say the very least, getting turned into ash."

Ash? No, thank you. "Why is she sure that person is me?"

Xara smiles. "I think we all know it."

She's right. Deep down, I know she is right. I just wish she wasn't.

"We need to make sure that Araz doesn't get to the Magic Of Nature," Obsidian says.

"Where is the Magic Of Nature hidden?" I ask.

"Everywhere! But my sister will try to collect it through the roots of the redwood trees. That is why she set up camp here in the first place," she says.

"We need to make sure that she won't use me to collect it. What do I need to do?" I ask Xara.

She smiles. "How good are you at smashing a Homaso?"

What? (In case you are wondering, Homaso stands for Holder Of Magic And Spirit Orb.)

"What do you mean?"

"Well, Araz has concentrated all of the magic she stole into a Homaso. If you can break it, then all the magic will be released back into the air, my sister won't be able to use it, the storm should break, *and* everyone who lost their magic would soak it back in and the stone would melt off of them like snow would melt off of your glove."

"Hmm. It is a good plan," I admit.

"Yes! Xara and I can distract Araz while you break the Homaso!" Obsidian says.

"Where is the Homaso kept?"

"In a cage full of magic-infused weeping willow tree branches. The strongest cage ever."

Wait, why is there a weeping willow in the redwood forest?

We talk back and forth about a plan until at last we come up with one that makes defeat seem not so imminent.

"Alright. Let's do it," I finally relent.

Obsidian and Xara cheer.

"But we need a backup plan. Like, what do I do if you can't distract her long enough?" I ask.

They stop cheering.

"Or what if she tries to collect the magic again?"

"Hmm. Did Acari give you anything that could help?" Obsidian asks.

Oh! The amber! "She did give me this. I think I can use it to call her."

"Perfect, we distract, you break, and if anything goes wrong, we call Acari! Perfect plan," he says.

I sigh. "You and I have very different definitions of 'perfect' Obsidian."

He grins. "Well, we only need one so we are going with my definition. Do you remember all the hiding spots?"

I scan the illusion one last time. "Yep. Got it all right here!"

"Perfect! Let's go!" Xara starts typing coordinates into the Ttufos machine.

"Wait, shouldn't we like, run through the plan one more time? Or come up with a plan C? Or-"

"Stop stalling Lyra! Let's go!" Obsidian says, grabbing hold of the Ttufos.

Lightning bolts. I think he pulled that from my head.

"Yep, I sure did pull the fact that you were stalling from your head. Now let's stop wasting time and go!"

I take a deep breath. He's right. Time to stop wasting time and go!

I grab onto the Ttufos machine. "Let's go stop Araz!"

Xara pushes a button and we rip straight through the fabric of the universe, landing right outside Araz's camp.

Chapter Twenty: Well, We Completely Left Him Out

This time, we do not in fact, land on top of each other. So far so good!

"Communication through the mind only, you guys know what to do," Obsidian's voice comes through in my head.

We all nod.

"Move out!" Xara exclaims to my mind.

I cringe. She still hasn't figured out how to control her volume.

They slip away from me quietly to not give away where I am hiding and appear on the opposite side of camp.

"Hey Araz!" Obsidian calls.

She startles and jumps up from talking to a redwood root, no doubt trying to extract the Magic Of Nature from it.

"Hello there, I was wondering when you were going to be brave enough to come back."

Xara smiles. "I see you did not take my suggestion on changing the color of your hair dear sister."

That was the code for me to start moving. I quietly start making my way towards the weeping willow tree, the shadows in the forest concealing my figure.

Creeping closer and closer, I start to think that I might actually be able to do this.

I repeat to myself over and over again until the weeping willow cage holding the Homaso is right in front of me. I still don't understand why there would be a willow tree in the redwoods though.

I risk a quick glance at my friends who are darting and weaving around Araz's lightning bolts.

I really want to say, "Nothing can stop me now!" but, you know what happens right after you say it.

I crouch down and feel the roots of the tree, and telepathically send a message to it saying, "Please open up. I won't hurt you."

But something is off about the tree. Its energy feels weird. Evil almost. Or like a Human.

I frown and stand up. That is when it happens. The tree quickly... unravels. That is the closest word I can find. It quickly unravels itself and turns into Camo!

Lightning bolts. We completely forgot about him.

"Did you seriously think that Zara would hide such a valuable thing in such an obvious spot? Oh no! She hid it somewhere where you will never find it!"

I groan inwardly. Not this guy again.

"Zara trusted me so much that she had me pretend to be a fake Homaso and she had no doubt that I wouldn't fail her to capture you. Now, your friends are going to lose their magic and you will take the Magic Of Nature for Zara and then she and I will rule this galaxy and beyond. Those Humans think we aren't real. Hah! We'll show them! We'll rule over them and take away their homes just like they took away ours! They will never say that we don't exist. They erased us from the history books when we gave them everything they needed to grow their gardens and survive. We were slaves of fear. Now, they will face the same enslavement that we have endured all these years!"

Yada, yada, yada! I can't tell if this is true or if he just likes the sound of his own voice. The fewer Humans that believe in magic the smaller amount of energy our life trees get. Our life forces are connected to our life tree and our life trees get energy from Humans believing in the Magic Of Nature. And last I checked, no one lived in fear, at least not when the village was full. Everyone was always celebrating, well, everything!

I decide that he just likes the sound of his own voice. That lines up with what Acari told me. I gasp as I realize that she has given me the answer on how to deal with Camo.

He smirks. "Didn't know that, did you?"

Huh? Oh! He thinks that I am still listening. I shake my head, which he takes as a cue to gloat. Really, I am shaking my head at the thought that he thinks I believe a word he says.

"Wow. You sure know a lot, don't you? I am very impressed. You must be very trustworthy for... *Zara*... to trust you with the hiding spot of the Homaso. I bet she would trust no one else," I say, reaching out to Obsidian to see how he is doing.

No response. That isn't good. I shake myself and listen to Camo.

"Oh yes! She would have never EVER trusted anyone else with the hiding spot of the Homaso."

"She hid it well I presume?"

He looks at me, annoyed. "I just told you that five seconds ago. Yes, she hid it very well. In a place only she could access."

"I heard you are a very good camishift."

"The best!" He smirks.

"I don't think so. Can you turn into a Frost Flower?" I ask.

"Yeah, I can!"

"Prove it!"

"Okay, I will!" He hunches his shoulders and shifts into a Frost Flower. I am secretly impressed but keep my expression blank.

He shifts back. "Good enough?" he asks.

"It's okay I guess," I say, pretending to examine my nail. "But you know what only the most extreme Camishifts would be able to shift into? The place where one would keep a Homaso. I have never, ever seen anyone do a correct impersonation of that. I bet you can't either."

"Yes I can!" he cries indignantly. He stretches his arms over his head and he turns into a perfect replica of a redwood tree. However, something is off about it. I just can't put my finger on it.

He shifts back. "That good enough for you? That was a perfect replica of where Zara keeps her Homaso hidden-" he claps his hands over his mouth and horror draws across his face as it dawns on him what he just said.

I realize that when I was following Illusion Araz, she led me right to the Homaso's hiding spot.

I turn and break into a run with Camo hot on my heels. He changes into an eagle and soars above me. I twist around and try to pelt him down with hail the size of baseballs. One hits him on the head and he goes crashing down. Good. That should buy me some time.

I send a quick message to Obsidian and get no response. I try Xara. Nothing.

I think back to the tree Camo turned into, trying to remember any distinguishing feature. This means that I don't see where I am going and trip on a root. That in turn breaks my concentration on my hailstorm.

I push myself up but am too late and Camo tackles me.

"Get off!" I shout as I roll over and blast him with a gust of wind.

He goes flying and I finally spot the tree I need to get to. It has the same tiny hole at the base. Now that I get a good look at it, I realize that it is losing its leaves which is very strange for a redwood tree considering they are evergreens. That is what seemed off about the tree!

I run as hard as I can, boosting myself with my wind.

Finally, I reach the tree. I crouch down and whisper to it telepathically. *"Please let me in. I need to save my friends."*

The tree responds by shuddering and untwisting to reveal a hidden door. I dash through before Camo can catch up to me. The tree quickly closes behind me, locking me in and everyone else out.

Ominous, right?

Chapter Twenty-One: Destroying The Homaso

Once inside, I sit down and catch my breath.

As I look around for the Homaso, I try contacting my friends one last time. Still silence. I guess that means they were captured and put back into that magic-proof house thing/prison.

I can't let my friends' sacrifice be in vain so I must destroy the Homaso.

That is if I can find it.

It looks as though Araz has been living here. There is a sleeping bag on the floor and on the desk, there is a paper with all her research on the Magic Of Nature.

I continue to look around as quickly as I can. Suddenly, I hear Araz outside, shouting at Camo.

I need to hurry! The bark starts to unravel, and I haven't even found the Homaso!

"Please, please, please don't let her in!" I plead.

The redwood tree must hear me because the tree starts to close up.

I hear Araz's angry shouts as the tree keeps raveling himself up.

"Thank you!" I message, and start to quickly rummage through all the research papers. Nothing.

I run my hands over the bark, looking for a hidden compartment. Nothing! Where is the Homaso hidden?

I check the desk for any clues. There is an important-looking paper with instructions to a person called Amaranth but nothing else that seems important. I tuck it into my pocket for later.

"What are you looking for?" a voice from behind asks.

I jump and twist around in the air, fully prepared to blast them with a hailstorm.

But when I land, I see it is only a young boy- no older than eight years of age.

"Who are you?" I ask.

"The spirit of this tree. Have you come to free me from the Evil Girl?"

"Um, yes?" As soon as I say that, I know it is the right answer because his face lights up like a fire. "Um, how do I do that?"

"Easy! Keeping the Homaso safe is draining my energy. All you have to do is destroy it, and I will finally have the energy to kick that girl out!"

I laugh. "I like your attitude! But where is the Homaso kept?"

"Up there of course!"

I look up. Way, way, *way* up.

Hanging about thirty-five feet above our heads is a weeping willow cage with the biggest Homaso I have ever seen inside.

"That is real, correct? Like, it is not someone pretending to be a cage?"

The boy nods. "Yes. I have been watching it day and night, waiting for someone like you to come along and free it. I would know if it was a fake."

"How do I get up there?"

"You climb!" the boy says as if the answer is obvious. In a way, I guess it is the obvious answer, except I don't think I can climb a tree from the *inside* of it. Still, I try to no avail. The bark is very loosely connected on the inside and the second I try to climb; the bark rips off and I fall down.

"Is there any other way up? Like a ladder or branches?"

He shakes his head. "Not unless you can fly."

Hmm. I can't fly, but I *can* boost myself up with my wind.

That gives me an idea that is dangerous and highly likely to fail for anyone but myself.

I climb up onto the desk and count down from three in my head. *Three! Two! One!* I jump up with all my strength and just as I start to fall, I boost myself up using short bursts of wind.

Finally, with one last burst of wind, I reach the cage. I grab hold of the bars with what little strength I have left and plead with the branches to let the Homaso go. Surprisingly, they relent fairly quickly, unlike every other willow I have ever met. The branches unravel and I swipe up the Homaso and get ready to go down. I take a moment to catch my breath and get ready to jump. I let go and jump. I try to use my wind to break my fall, but I am too tired from using my wind to get up.

I fall on my back but don't have time to register the pain before I slip into darkness, the young boy shouting my name. I don't know how he got it. I really should have asked him his . . .

I wake up an hour later (according to my watch which has seen so much water it is a miracle it still works) to find the boy crouching over my body, cleaning a cut I must have gotten when I fell.

I groan and sit up, ignoring the pain in my back. I look around for the Homaso and spot it on the ground, a few feet away.

"Are you okay Lyra?" he asks, his voice tight with concern.

I nod and his shoulders sag in relief.

"How did you know my name?" I ask.

"Alaani told me. Our roots are like your weathernet or the Human's internet. Connecting us all."

"What is your name?"

"Sev," he says.

"Nice to meet you Sev. Would you happen to know how to safely destroy this thing?" If you don't destroy one safely, that person's spirit will take your magic for itself.

"First, you soak the orb in warm water. Then, when its outside feels grainy and lights turn from yellow and blue to green and purple, you smash it on a spiritine crystal and the magic will be released."

"Where the weather am I supposed to find a spiritine crystal?"

"Here." Sev reaches into his pocket and pulls out a spiritine crystal, it's baby blue and sunset orange lights bouncing around as though they were laughing or dancing.

I stare at it until Sev clears his throat. "Hmm?" I ask, still mesmerized by the crystal.

"There is a tub over there and I can warm up some water for you if you like," he says.

"That would be great!" I get up to grab the tub but fall back down instantly. Guess my legs aren't ready to walk yet. Still, I try again, and this time I manage to walk over to the tub.

I bring it back and set it on the ground. Then I pick up the Homaso, dust it off, and put it in the tub.

"Over here!" Sev calls. I look up and see him whispering to the tree.

Roots shoot up, weaving together to create a beautiful fountain-looking creation.

"Ask the tree for warm water," Sev says.

"Aren't you the spirit of the tree? Can't I just ask you?"

"Just ask the tree!"

I sigh, still exhausted from using the wind. Ignoring my sore muscles, I push myself off the ground and bring the tub over to where Sev is waiting for me.

"*Excuse me, um, Sequoia sempervirens?*" I ask, using the tree's proper name to show respect. "*Would you mind sparing a tiny bit of water and heating it up and pouring it in here? Thank you!*" I stop and wait.

The roots start shaking and suddenly, water comes gushing out of the roots, filling the tub instantly.

"*That's enough, thank you!*" I say, but the water keeps coming.

"*Thank you!*" I yell, louder this time. The water flow abruptly cuts off and the roots sink back into the ground.

"How long do I let this soak?"

"About an hour."

"An hour!"

"Why don't you rest?" Sev suggests gently.

"I don't... have... time *YAWN* to rest..." But before I know what I am doing, I lay down on the ground and slip into a deep, heavy, dreamless sleep.

I awaken an hour later to find Sev walking over to me.

"Ah good! You're awake! I was just going to wake you. Come check out the Homaso. It is starting to turn green and purple."

He leads me over to the tub.

The Homaso is now radiating neon green and purple lights.

"Wow," I breathe.

"Where is the spiritine?" I ask, half distracted by the light show going on, created by the Homaso's light bouncing around as if dancing to music only it can hear.

Sev shakes himself, him too being mesmerized by the lights. He reaches into a pocket and pulls out the crystal. "Here you go."

I take it and bury a quarter of it in the ground.

I gently rub three fingers against the Homaso, confirming the grainy texture. As I rub my fingers against it, I can hear the faint cries of the people whose magic is trapped. Amongst them, I can make out my family. I realize I can't hear Ateil's voice. I didn't see her in the group of stone people either. Hmm. A mystery for later. One thing at a time. First, I need to free all of these people.

With shaky hands, I lift the Homaso and poise it over the spiritine. Then, I hesitate. Sev notices and asks what's up.

"Do you want to do the honors?" I ask.

Sev's eyes widen and he nods.

I hand the Homaso over to him and he takes it in his tiny eight-year-old hands. He reminds me of my brother. A wave of sadness crashes into me as he lifts it over his head and brings it crashing down on the spiritine.

The Homaso makes a metallic ringing sound accompanied by a blinding light the color of a sunset.

Sev and I cringe, covering our eyes, not that it does us any good.

Slowly, the light dies away and it is safe to lower our hands. I rub away the spots dancing in front of my eyes and confirm that the Homaso really is gone. It is! I take a deep breath and notice how the air smells like magic!

"Thank you!" I tell Sev, and I toss my arms around his neck, pulling him into a hug.

He seems surprised at first but then grins and hugs me back, nearly choking me.

I pull back and smile. "I wish you could join me," I say.

He gives me a sad smile in return.

"Don't worry about me. Thanks to you, I have enough energy to kick Evil Girl out now!" He winks and I laugh.

"Now where are you off to Lyra?" he asks.

I take a deep breath. "I'm off to free my friends. Then I'm going to confront Araz."

"Are your friends in the evil lifeless prison thing?"

"Yes."

"Then you will probably need this." He reaches into his back pocket and pulls out a Ttufos machine.

"How did you-"

He winks. "Just because I am a tree, doesn't mean I can't hear secrets or steal stuff!"

I giggle. "Thanks!" I call on the wind to tell me the coordinates of the prison and punch them into the Ttufos machine.

"Hey Lyra," Sev says. "After you defeat Evil Girl, will you come back and free me from my home?"

I look up at Sev's bright and hopeful face and can't find the words to say that I don't know how to. Instead, I say, "I will."

His face lights up and he runs over and wraps me up in his tiny eight-year-old arms. I scoop him up and hold him close. He really reminds me of my little brother. Just a year younger.

"Be careful," he whispers in my ear.

"I will." I set him down and push the button on the Ttufos machine. Time and space wrap around me as I get one last look at Sev's young and hopeful face. I *will* defeat Araz, no matter what it takes.

Chapter Twenty-Two: Family Reunion!

I arrive at the prison and stumble around in the darkness.

"Obsidian! Xara! Are you in here?" I whisper-yell.

I hear a figure in the darkness jump up. Suddenly, Xara and Obsidian are at my side.

"Is it really you?" Xara asks, narrowing her eyes.

I nod. "It really is me." Then to her mind. *"Trust me. I am not your sister."*

She grins. "I just need one last piece of proof. Tell us what happened."

Obsidian looks confused and then realizes that I talked to Xara's mind.

"Yeah! What happened out there Lyra?"

I sit down and tell them all about meeting Sev and breaking the Homaso. I don't tell them about the promise I made to Sev or not seeing Ateil. I don't need to worry them with those details.

"Wow," Obsidian says.

"What happened to you?" I ask.

"Well," Xara begins. "Araz basically just trapped us in a wind cell, and then Ttufosed us here."

"A wind cell?"

Obsidian nods.

"Hmm. I need to learn how to do that."

I think about how I could achieve that when I realize that my parents must be waking up right now!

Obsidian must be thinking the same thing because he shouts at the same time I do, "Our families!"

I pull out the Ttufos machine and hold it out to my friends. They grab a hold of it as I punch in the coordinates. "Ready?" I ask them. They nod. "Then let's go!"

I push the Ttufos button and space warps around us as we silently escape prison for the second time today.

We appear behind the rhododendron bush, amid a crowd of confused people. I scan through all of them, looking for my family.

As soon as I found out what had happened, I started dreaming of this moment. Sometimes I would arrive on a carriage, and everyone would bow down to me. Other times my family would be crying, and I would show up and surprise them all. Or I would be realistic and imagine me melting in their arms.

But none of that actually happens. Instead, I realize for the first time just how cold it is without the Sun's light.

Wait, where *is* the solid drop of light that powers the Sun? Does Araz have it?

I tip my head back and look up. The storm has stopped but the clouds still haven't dissipated. I decide to ignore that right now (though I am sure I will regret it) and turn my attention back to the mob of confused back-from-being-stone people.

It looks like losing their magic took a toll on the older people, for they are taking the longest to wake up. Not seeing my family, I look around for Araz. I think that she might have the drop of light somewhere on her. I hope she doesn't.

One tiny peek over the bush shows me Araz and Camo still trying to get into Sev. But he is right, he can handle this. I know this because right now, perhaps Sev sensed me watching, he decides to take matters into his own hands (roots) and shoots some roots up which grab them by their ankles and swing them around so they are not facing us.

"Put us down!" Araz shrieks.

Sev suddenly drops them onto the ground, and a sinkhole swallows them up.

Xara appears by my side. "Three guesses as to where *they* are going."

I laugh. Every child is taught the story of the great Eloh. A magic sinkhole that will appear when needed and sucks people into a desert they cannot escape. Parents would tell their children "Behave or Eloh will get you!" or "Don't disrespect Mother Nature or Eloh will come and suck you up!"

Well, it seems that Eloh came and got Araz. Oh, lightning bolts. I sure hope that she doesn't have the solid drop of light with her now!

"Hopefully that is the last we see of her!" I say.

Suddenly, I am attacked from behind! Only, it just feels like an attack. When I turn around, I realize it is my nine-year-old brother James!

"James!" I shout. I pick him up and squeeze him hard. He squeezes me back, nearly choking me.

"Not so tight!" I choke out. As soon as I set him down, the rest of my family scoops me up.

I give Mama, Papa, and my Tía Islana a big hug before they finally let me go.

"Sis, where are we? And what time is it? I am SO hungry," James complains.

I laugh at him. "You're always hungry!" I say, trying and failing to mess up his hair.

"Yes, he is. What did happen?" Papa asks.

"There is a lot I need to tell you all."

"Then tell us!" Islana insists.

"Okay. But you might want to sit down. This is a long and crazy story."

We all sit down and I start my story with Obsidian appearing at my front door. I tell them about the riddle, about Araz and Xara, about finding the Frost Flower and being its Guardian, about Sev, and how I broke the Homaso to free them.

"Amazing!" Islana says when I am done. "I think I might retire and write a book about your quest instead!"

"Aye! With what our daughter has told us, it seems as though you couldn't have taught her anything new anyway!" Papa jokes.

I laugh.

"Lyra!" I hear someone call. I turn towards the voice and see Obsidian standing with his grandparents, smiling and waving at me to walk over.

"Coming!" I call and stick my hands out for my brother to pull me up. "Pull me up, James!" I command.

He laughs as he grabs my hands and pulls me up.

"Thanks," I say.

We get up and head over to him and his grandparents. Mama and Papa talk with his grandparents who are on the Elders Council, filling them in on what Obsidian left out.

They suddenly drop their voices and I catch words and phrases like "still missing" and "Eloh" and "earring Homaso?" before they realize that Obsidian and I are eavesdropping and move away.

"Hmph! Considering we literally just brought them back from being stone, you would think we could handle what they are talking about," Obsidian complains.

"I think they were talking about Ateil," I say quietly.

He whirls around to face me. "What do you mean?"

"Find Xara. Then I can tell both of you."

We look around and finally find Xara off to the side, looking slightly uncomfortable at all the families rejoicing.

"Hey Xara, my master/ professor Ateil is still missing. I don't think that her magic was ever put into that Homaso I destroyed. Did you see anything mentioning her while you were snooping around your sister's stuff?"

She shakes her head. "Sorry, Lyra. Never heard of her."

I sigh. What the weather could have happened to her?

Obsidian nudges me. "Hey, if the adults don't know or won't tell us, then let's go find out for ourselves."

I smile. "You in Xara?"

"Oh yeah! Let's go find your missing master!"

I look around to make sure no one is watching us. Obsidian's grandparents and my family are filling everyone in on what happened. Looks like the coast is clear.

We quietly slip away from all the chaos, walking past the rhododendron bush and out towards Araz's camp.

"Funny how now that they are all free, they are still staying behind the rhododendron bush," Xara observes.

Just then, a little girl walks over to the edge of the bush, steps forward, and hits an invisible wall. She gets zapped, falls for a moment, then gets up, shrugs, and skips away like nothing happened.

"Okay, that was really weird," Obsidian says.

Xara and I nod. We watch as the same thing happens to a young boy and Obsidian's grandma Kirana from the Elders Council at Willow Academy.

"Why are we the only ones who can walk through?" I ask, not really expecting an answer.

As if it were shrugging, the ground starts to rumble. But when it keeps rumbling, I get a feeling that something very bad is going to happen.

"Earthquake!" Xara yells and we all dive for cover in an old burnt-out redwood stump.

"Look!" I shout. "They aren't affected at all!"

It was true. Not a single person seems to have been affected by the earthquake. In fact, they all seem quite oblivious to it.

Quite suddenly, the earthquake stops.

We wait a few heartbeats before crawling out and risk asking, "Is it over? Was that it?"

Then, the worst possible thing I can think of at this moment happens.

The ground fractures and splits open, creating a deep dark ravine, and the impossible happens.

The one person I never, EVER, want to see again shoots out of it.

No one has ever heard of anyone coming back from Eloh. But this isn't just anyone.

Yep. Araz is back. Lightning bolts. Isn't there like, a rule that villains can't come back after they have been defeated?

Well, apparently either Araz doesn't know that rule or she is just choosing to ignore it. Both are highly likely.

"Run!" Obsidian yells.

Xara takes off but doubles back when I don't follow. My feet feel glued to the ground so I am very grateful when Obsidian grabs the back of my shirt and practically drags me back into that old log.

Once we are safely inside, I telepathically ask the tree to close up leaving a tiny window. The tree happily obliges, having heard how I helped Sev kick out "that Evil Girl".

We wait in tense silence as we watch Araz look around until Xara finally breaks it by yelling "Um, what the weather just happened?!"

Um, yeah! What she said!

Chapter Twenty-Three: She's Baaaack!

"Yeah! What she said!" Obsidian explodes, echoing my thoughts. His hair starts turning into different colors and animal patterns. A sign that he is truly angry and terrified. And a sign I have only ever seen once on him when he told me that his mom and dad had gone missing on a mission into the Human world. He has never felt the same towards Humans after that.

"Be quiet!" I snap, though I also want to explode. "Araz can't see us, but she will most certainly hear you yelling if you keep it up."

Obsidian says nothing so that is good enough for me.

"Do you think that Araz will recapture your family's magic?" Xara asks, breaking the tense silence that had formed between all of us.

I peek out the window. Our families are *completely* oblivious to Araz's return.

"What the weather?!" Obsidian yells into my ear, peeking over my shoulder. "They don't even know she is back!"

"We need to get them out of there!" I say. "*Thank you for keeping us safe. Do you mind opening up?*"

The tree slowly starts to unravel but Xara holds me back before I can do anything.

"Wait. Do you have an *actual plan* on how to get everyone to safety?"

Wait- is she seriously asking me if I have a plan when she wouldn't even triple-check our old one?

I groan. "No, but we have to do something!"

I am fully prepared to charge out when Obsidian holds me back. I sigh.

Apparently, I am not allowed to do anything until I satisfy their ravenous craving for a decent plan. Okay, now that I say it to myself, that does sound kind of smart.

"Do you still have that gift from Acari?" Obsidian asks.

I reach into my satchel and pull it out.

"Perfect, 'cause I think I have an idea."

After a beat of silence, Xara asks, "Well are you going to tell us what it is or are we just going to have to guess or are we just going to sit around and wait while my sister kidnaps your family?"

"Hey Xara, what about your family?" I ask, surprised that I just remembered right now that she has never mentioned anything about her family. (Besides Zara).

"Long story, I'll tell you later. Now about that plan?"

Hmm. That was not an answer. I need to remember to grill her about that later. Obsidian's voice pulls me from my thoughts.

"Right. Lyra, you call Acari and she can rescue everyone while we face off with Araz. Easy!"

"Not only do we have different definitions of 'perfect' we also have completely opposite definitions of the word 'easy'," I say.

He shrugs.

"Um, my sister? Remember?" Xara asks, pulling us back on track.

"Right." I pull the amber out of my satchel.

"Um, do either of you know how to work this thing?" I ask.

"It's your amber," Obsidian says unhelpfully.

"Well, it's not like it came with an instruction manual," I grumble. "Not a clue?"

They both shake their heads. I guess that they didn't exactly teach us how to use a piece of magical amber to call a worm queen to help us at school.

"Maybe try closing your eyes, squeezing it, and calling for help with your mind?" Xara suggests.

Not having any better ideas, I take her suggestion.

I reach my mind out to the amber, listening for anything. Then, I pick up a faint signal.

"Hello! Acari? Are you there?" I ask.

"Lyra?"

"Yes, it is me. Araz, that is what we call Zara, just escaped Eloh and now she is going to try to take back everyone's magic. We need your help. Can you get our friends and family out safely for us?"

A sigh. *"I am guessing that a lot happened after I left?"*

"Yes, I will explain later but we desperately need your help. Please!"

I hold my breath, waiting for Acari's response.

"I'm on my way."

I let my breath out and turn to my friends.

"She's coming."

They let out their breath as well.

"Let's go distract Araz until Acari gets here," Xara says.

We nod and I go out first, no one stopping me this time.

I scan the area for Araz. I finally spot her arguing with Sev. When he doesn't budge, she throws her hands up and starts stomping over to our families.

"She's heading towards our families!" I report and they rush out.

We sprint across the field, trying to catch up with Araz.

Mama notices me running towards her and she smiles and waves. Then, her eyes go glassy for a second and she shakes herself as if waking up from a dream. Her eyes widen in horror. I guess she can see Araz now.

"*We're fine. Get everyone one in a single file line, help is on the way!*" I tell her.

She bites her lip and then nods. She turns and starts yelling instructions at everyone.

There is chaos as everyone breaks through the mental fog and sees Araz moving towards them.

Araz is almost over there so I fling my arms in her direction, pelting her with hail the size of golf balls.

"Ahh!" she yells, trying to swat the storm away.

Just then, the ground begins to rumble, and I wonder if Camo is coming back as well. But then Acari breaks through the Earth, much bigger than she was before.

She turns, intentionally or unintentionally swatting Araz fifty feet away with her giant tail. She tunnels underground and comes up on the other side then lifts her whole body above ground, lifting everyone who was standing in the line onto her humongous body.

"Get them out of here!" I shout.

"What about you Sis?" James asks.

I smile and shove my satchel at him. "I'll be back when Araz is gone."

Everyone on Acari starts to protest but she tunnels underground, and no one is brave enough to jump off.

I flip my braid over my shoulder and turn back to my friends. "Well, I guess all that is left is to end this war. Let's go."

Chapter Twenty-Four: Ending The Fight Is A Lot Harder Than They Make It Seem In The Movies

We all turn around, ready to face Araz who is slowly drawing herself up from the mud pile Acari had flung her into.

We start walking towards her. If this was a TV show, we would be walking very slowly, with dramatic music playing. But I'm not much for all that type of stuff so I'll skip over the walking over part because we *are* walking over slowly, however, there is not any dramatic music playing and if there was, I would pelt the speakers with lightning until it all stopped.

We cross half the camp and are surprised to find Araz, standing in the middle of a small clearing, clearly waiting for us. The clearing was literally a clearing. It was clear of everything. Of mud, grass, trees, and roots. Just a bare patch of dirt, not too far from where Araz got tossed.

"Well?" she asks.

"Well what?" I ask, confused.

She throws her hands up like the answer should be obvious.

"Are you going to join me or not? If you aren't, then why did you ditch your only chance to escape?"

Is this girl serious right now?! I look straight into her jade-green eyes. Yep. She's dead serious.

I sigh, then straighten my shoulders and force myself to look back into her eyes.

"No Zara," I say, using her proper name even though I really want to annoy her so I can get a reason to toss her into another mud hole. "We are not here to join you. We are here to fix your mistakes, whether you help us or not." I pause, then take a risk that never ever works out. "You can still fix it, you know. We'll help. Join us." I hold my breath, waiting for her to laugh. Instead, her shoulders just slump as she sighs. Then, she rolls them back and looks straight at me.

"I can see how you think this is a mistake. But it is not. Fixing it will ruin everything. And you obviously won't join me so I guess the only option is for you to leave me alone."

What? She better not expect us to just leave. Then I notice her lip is slightly curved upward.

This is a trick.

Obsidian steps forward, no doubt a retort as sharp as the volcanic glass he is named after already on his tongue, but I stop him.

"*It's a trick,*" I say. "*Let it go.*"

He sighs and nods.

"Well, you did not take my bait so this should get interesting."

"Yes, it will. Because we will get some interesting answers. Now where is she?" I demand.

"Who?" Zara asks, feigning innocence.

"Ateil," I snarl.

"And the solid drop of light that you stole from the Sun!" Xara adds.

I jump. I'd completely forgotten she was here!

Zara smirks. "Well, since you asked so rudely, I suppose I can show you."

Since you asked so rudely? What? Since when do people respond when you ask them for something rudely?

Zara draws my attention back to her as something on her catches my eye. She slowly draws her fiery red hair back away from her ears. I've always wondered why she kept her hair like that. And that's when I see them. Two giant earrings. They had been completely concealed by her enormous amount of hair. On one earring is a Homaso. Not just any Homaso, Ateil's. I can tell because it is shining the same amethyst color that Ateil's eyes used to be. On the other is a teardrop shape of light, its brightness dimming by the second.

"Give them to us," I demand, though I know she won't.

She smirks. "Come and get them."

"With pleasure!" I say, glancing at my friends.

We really need a plan here! Obsidian moves to my right side with Xara on my left.

"Since we have to fight to get the earrings, may as well make it fun!" Obsidian whispers to us.

I fight back a laugh, deciding if I want to hug him or strangle him. Unfortunately, or fortunately, I can't do both if we have to fight to defeat Zara. Only Obsidian could think of a fight as "fun".

We stand still, with Zara circling us. Everyone waiting for another person to make the first move.

Finally, Zara runs out of patience and leaps at us.

Suddenly, my body knows what to do as I am filled with adrenaline.

I drop and roll out of the way of her attack, springing back up to my feet much faster than her. I hurl a hailstorm at her, slowing her next attack which is directed at her sister.

"Obsidian, change into something I can fling at her," I command.

"You better know what you are doing!" is his only response as he runs towards me and shifts into a short staff.

"Perfect!" I say, and whisper to him my plan.

"I can't distract her much longer!" Xara's voice comes in my head.

I give her a slight nod and raise my arms above my head, hailing the largest storm I have ever made. No wait- not a storm, a hurricane.

The twins stop fighting to see where all the wind is coming from.

I concentrate and make the hurricane as small as I can. It tries to escape my grasp, sensing the evil and wanting to destroy it, but I hold it back.

"Watch out!" I warn Xara. Then I release my grip on the hurricane and it goes flying towards Zara.

Xara has time to dive out of the way because of my warning but Zara only has time for her eyes to widen (bad decision considering all the dust the hurricane is picking up) before it captures her in its grasp.

"Ready?" I ask Obsidian. He can't answer because he is a staff, but the staff warms in my hands. "I'll take that as a yes!"

I run towards the hurricane, creating a blockade around me with some wind. It protects me from all the dust, but not the rain. I think that I don't ever want to see rain again after this!

I jump into the hurricane and look around for Zara. Finally, I spot her, her eyes red from all the dust.

I use the wind to surround me with a shield of dust so Zara can't see me coming, not that she could see me anyway. It whips my braid around, smacking me in the face. I shove it out of my face and look at Zara.

I wait until Zara's back is towards us. "Here we go!" I tell Obsidian, hoping that my plan works.

"Three."

I lower my blockade.

"Two."

I aim Obsidian.

"One!"

I toss Obsidian and watch him go flying towards Zara. I boost him with my wind.

Right before he hits Zara in the back of the head, he shifts back into himself and tackles Zara to the ground.

She shrieks but doesn't have the energy to fight him.

I sprint over and gently pull the earrings off of her ears.

I put them in my satchel and stop the storm. I lay back and close my eyes, exhausted.

"Good job Lyra!" I open my eyes to find Obsidian standing over me grinning. He offers his hand and I take it, knowing that we still aren't safe.

"Well, well, well. Aren't you exhausted?" Zara asks.

We turn. Zara is standing up, her knees only a little wobbly, much better than I am doing.

"I see you got my earrings, well yo-" she is cut off as someone ties a sweatshirt around her head, gagging her. They swing their leg out and around, knocking Zara over.

We look up to find Xara standing over her sister.

"Sorry, I was really getting tired of hearing her voice."

"What do we do with her now?" Obsidian asks.

"I don't know," Xara answers.

They both turn to me. I close my eyes. What do we do with her?

The Frost Flower, a voice in my mind says. My eyes jerk open. That voice wasn't mine or Xara's or Obsidians. Whose voice was it? It sounded familiar. Almost like an ocean wave... I listen but I can't hear it anymore so after a few more tries I give up and realize that they are still waiting for me.

I look down at Zara. Could the voice be right? As I watch her wriggle like a worm, I know it is. Zara just poses too big a threat.

I pull the Frost Flower from my pocket with shaky hands.

Obsidian's eyes widen as he realizes what I am going to do.

Xara's eyes fill with tears. She leans down and whispers something that sounds like "I love you!" to Zara and then stands and nods to me.

I take a deep breath and roll Zara over so I can look into her eyes.

"I don't want to do this, but you have given us no choice. I'm sorry. I truly am."

With that, I close my eyes and give all my strength to the Frost Flower, suddenly knowing what to do.

I give up all my sadness, my anger, my hope, my triumph, and my happiness. I feed it to the Frost Flower.

Then, I picture Zara's face.

Her cold jade green eyes, her red hair that looks like lava. And I direct the Frost Flower to it.

There is a light so blinding I can see it very clearly even though my eyes are closed and once it dissipates, I know that Zara is encased in ice for the next few thousand years. Nothing can break the ice of a Frost Flower. Nothing.

I hear the ground rumble as Eloh opens up beneath Zara and swallows her. Most likely taking her to Acratana. The real Antarctica.

I hear Obsidian's shouts of triumph and Xara's sobs, but I can't focus on anything.

I don't open my eyes. I can't open my eyes. I should be terrified by that prospect, but I am just too tired, and my eyes feel like paperweights.

Then I hear their shouts and sobs turn to voices of concern as they notice that I am not doing anything.

I begin to sway and fall when someone holds me or catches me. I don't know which. I am just so tired!

I think I might fall asleep for a little while...

Yeah, sleep, that sounds good...

I think I will just ignore my friends and fall asleep...

That sounds nice...

Really nice...

Chapter Twenty-Five: Home Sweet Home

I dream about Zara encased in ice, I hear Xara crying and Obsidian worrying. I can't tell if they are a part of the dream or not.

I hear someone say, "I think she is coming around." There is a bunch of rustling, and I finally have the strength to open my eyes.

I squint as lights blind my eyes, causing spots to dance across my vision. I close my eyes briefly and open them again and this time the lights are more tolerable.

As the world and my senses come into focus, I realize that I am lying down on my bed with familiar faces surrounding me. James, Mama, Papa, Islana, Obsidian, and Xara.

"What happened?" I ask. However, my tongue is not quite working properly so it sounds more like *"Whadahapen?"*

Thankfully, they can understand me and I get some answers.

"I don't know. One moment there was a searing blinding light, then Zara was encased in ice and then Eloh opened up and Xara and I were celebrating and then I realized that you weren't and you were looking all faint-like and Xara asked if you were okay and you responded by turning nearly as pale as the ice Zara is encased in and then you fainted and I caught you then Xara went and got help and well, here you are!" Obsidian explains in one big breath.

"Wow. How long have I been out?"

"Two and a half days," Islana says.

My eyes widen. Two whole days!

Mama smiles. "Your brother hasn't left your side in twenty-four hours."

"Thanks, J. What happened to everyone else? And Zara?"

"Zara is in Eloh and everyone else is settling back into their normal life. In fact, my grandparents are out giving instructions on how to rebuild the academy right now!" Obsidian exclaims.

We might get to go to school again? Awesome!

"So, when are you going to tell us what happened?!" Papa asks.

"Oh, yeah!" I tell them about my hurricane, taking the earrings from Zara, hearing a voice in my head telling me what to do, and how I gave all my energy to the Frost Flower.

"Wow," is the whole response that I get from everyone.

"Wait. A voice?" Mama asks.

"Yes. It sounded like the same person who told me that I am the Guardian of the Frost Flower."

"Hmm."

"Drink this." Islana pours a thick sweet honey-like liquid down my throat. Not only is she my professor, but she is also one of five doctors of the Magic People.

"Where did you put those evil earrings?" Obsidian asks.

"In my satchel," I say. I'd completely forgotten about them.

Obsidian moves to get it, but Xara beats him to it, glad to have something to do.

She hands it to me and I rummage through it. Finally, I find where I hid them.

"Here they are!"

One earring is shining a dim amethyst light but the other looks worse. It is a teardrop-shaped earring that is a honey color. It barely has any glow at all.

"Should it look like that?" Xara asks.

Islana shakes her head. "No, but I don't know what to do. Ateil would know, however."

"How do we free her?" Papa asks.

Everyone turns to me.

"What?"

"How did you free the other Homaso?" Mama asks.

"I had a little help." Sev! I forgot that I owe him a favor! "Tia, how do you free a tree spirit from its home?"

"Why?"

"If you give me the answer, I think I might be able to free Ateil."

"Well, if you infuse scissors with spiritine, you can cut the thread that binds them to the tree and they will be free."

"Perfect." I toss back the covers and go and get dressed, despite everyone's protests.

"Where are you going?" Papa asks.

"Nowhere I won't be safe." It is not the answer he is looking for but if I tell him the truth, everyone will most likely bind me to my bed.

I swipe the Ttufos machine off my lampstand and type in the coordinates.

"Be right back!" I say.

"Wait, you will need these scissors!" Islana says, handing me a pair.

Oops. I completely forgot.

"Thanks!" I tuck them into my sweatshirt pocket and Ttufos away before they can find another reason to stop me.

Chapter Twenty-Six: Repaying A Promise

As soon as I reach the abandoned camp, I realize that this is the first time that I have been outside in two and a half days.

I look up at the sky. It is dark out. But there are no clouds!

We do need to fix that Sun. One problem at a time though.

I run up to the base of Sev and ask him to open up. He unravels fairly quickly and I rush in to find him empty!

"Looks much better in here, right?" Sev asks from behind me.

I whirl around. "Sev!" I cry and he rushes into my arms.

"You came back! Do you think that you can free me? Is the world rid of Evil Girl?"

I laugh at the nickname. "Yes, the world is free of 'Evil Girl'. And yes, I have come to free you. Do you think you can do me a favor in return though?"

"Sure, what?"

"I need you to help me safely destroy a Homaso so I can bring back my master."

"Of course. Now can you free me?" He is so excited that he starts bouncing all over the place.

"Sure, if you can sit still for one minute!" I say.

He plops down in front of me.

"Do you still have the spiritine?" I ask, pulling the scissors from my pocket.

He nods and hands me the tiny, shiny crystal.

I take the crystal and rub it back and forth across the sharp end of the scissors, infusing them with its magic. Then I peek around him looking for, what did Islana call it again? The thread that binds him to the tree.

"What are you looking for?" Sev asks.

"According to my Tía Islana, I should be able to find the thread that connects you to this tree and if I cut that thread with these spiritine-infused scissors, then you should be free."

"Oh. The thread is right here." He reaches into his jeans pocket and pulls out a thread that seems to be connected to his chest.

"You keep your life's thread in the back of your jeans pocket?" Wow, this boy really wants to leave. If I were him, I would have put it into a lightning bolt-proof pocket that was hidden in the front of my shirt where I could always have it in my line of sight

He shrugs. "Can you cut the thread now? I've been waiting fifty years for this!"

"Fifty years?! You look like you are barely eight!"

"This is my Human/Magic People form."

Okay. No clue what any of that means but okay.

I move to cut the thread but hesitate.

"What is it?"

"If I cut this thread, it won't kill you, right?"

"Hmm. I never really thought about that. I mean, I do get my energy from the tree but it's still worth a shot. Go for it!"

Seriously? He *really* wants to leave.

"Okay. If you say so."

He holds up the thread to my scissors, I close my eyes and slowly close the scissors, not opening my eyes until I hear the thread break.

Then I ask Sev a bunch of questions to make sure he is okay.

"You're sure you are feeling okay?" I ask. He nods but he does look a little faint.

"I think I just need some Sun," he says.

That makes sense. I ask the tree to unravel and we step outside before I remember that there is no Sun.

"Hey, where did the Sun go?" Sev asks.

"I will explain everything soon. Just let me see one thing." I run over to where I had encased Zara in ice, but I find nothing but some upturned soil. Let's hope that this time she stays in Eloh.

"Can we go?" Sev asks. His teeth start chattering.

"Sure," I say. I frown at him and take off my sweatshirt. "Here, you need it more than I do."

He gratefully puts on the sweatshirt while I type the coordinates to my house into the Ttufos machine.

"Ready?" I ask.

He nods and clings to me.

"Then let's go!"

We Ttufos and can't get to my house soon enough because Sev nearly loses his grip on me several times. I can't really blame him though. I mean, would *you* expect a tree spirit to know how to Ttufos? In fact, I bet that you are a Human and probably don't know how to Ttufos. You probably don't even think we are real!

But back to my story. (Which *is* a true story. I hear that Obsidian is going to write his own, which, by the way, is totally inaccurate!)

Chapter Twenty-Seven: Freeing The Earring (That Sounds Weird)

We finally arrive back in my bedroom. Sev lets go of me and stumbles. I catch him before he can fall back down.

"Thanks," he whispers, clinging to my hand.

"Who's this?" Obsidian asks.

I look up and find everyone staring at me. "Everyone, this is Sev. He is who you have to thank for your freedom. He had the spiritine."

"Hi Sev!" Xara says.

"Nice to meet you Sev," all the adults say.

He greets them with a shy wave and shivers.

"Oh! You must be freezing. Here, take this Sun orb. I trapped a bit of Sunlight in it a long time ago for Lyra so she could read at night but I'm sure she doesn't mind sharing," Islana says, handing him the small light.

He takes it in his trembling hands and instantly stops shivering.

"How about we pin it to you?" I suggest.

"Good idea!" Islana takes out a hairpin from her hair and uses it to fasten the Sun orb to the front of Sev's (previously mine) sweatshirt.

"Thank you. I hear that you need help freeing a Homaso?"

"Ah, yes! Do you think you have the energy for that?" Mama asks.

Sev nods.

"Fantastic. Xara, can you bring it over here?" she asks.

Xara gets up and hands Ateil's Homaso to Sev.

"What do you need?" Papa asks.

"A tub, some warm water, and the spiritine crystal that I gave Lyra," Sev lists. They are the same things we used for the big Homaso.

James jumps up off of my bed and races out, coming back with a tub full of warm water.

"Thanks!" Sev takes the tub and puts it on my floor. He puts the earring in the warm water and sits down to wait.

"How long do we wait?" I ask, itching to get this over with.

"About five minutes. The other Homaso took longer because it held so much magic."

I nod and sit down. Funny how when you dread something, five minutes is five seconds, and when you are waiting for something, five minutes feels like five hours.

After checking my watch for the fifth time in the first minute, James asks something I have always wondered about but never asked before. His voice is a nice break from the silence that had fallen over us.

"Hey Mama, why do we call ourselves Magic People if magic isn't real?"

"Good question. 'Magic' is just a term that Humans use to describe something they don't understand. However, everything is magic if you think about it. But the term 'Magic People' came from when two of our people accidentally got caught doing 'magic' in front of a Human and the Human called us Magic People. So that is why we call ourselves Magic People. It is also because we can 'harness' the 'magic' of Nature. Since we adopted the Human's language, we don't have a better term than 'magic,'" Mama explains.

Okay? I think I understand.

"Five minutes is up!" Sev announces.

Finally!

I hand Sev the spiritine crystal and he holds it in between his feet.

"Wait, where is Ateil? I mean, we might free her, but we still don't know where she actually is," Obsidian points out.

Oh. He does make a good point.

"If I remember correctly, when Ateil was a baby, the Elders deemed her very powerful. They knew that people would try to take her Homaso so they put a piece of her in her own Homaso so if her Homaso was ever captured and freed when it was freed, the Homaso would turn into Ateil," Papa recalls.

"Do we need to do anything differently?" Xara asks.

"I don't think so?" Sev replies, though it sounds more like a question than a statement.

"Well, it's worth a shot!" I say.

Sev nods and pulls out Ateil's amethyst-colored, glittering Homaso. He raises it over his head and prepares to hit it when he pauses and says, "Do you want to do it Lyra?"

"Sure." I take the Homaso from Sev, raise it over my head, and bring it smashing down on the spiritine.

There's a flash of blinding violet light and the Homaso starts breaking apart into minuscule pieces. They float together, slowly forming Ateil's shape. They keep building and piling on top of one another when with a final burst of light, Ateil is finally standing right in front of me for the first time in two years.

She stumbles and falls onto my bed. "Woah! What the weather just happened?"

"Ateil!" I fly over to her and knock her back onto my bed, hugging her.

She laughs and hugs me back, her forest green hair falling in her face. "I guess I missed something important?"

"You have no idea." Before I can further elaborate, there is a knock on the front door.

"I'll get it!" Before anyone can stop him, James is flying out of my bedroom and we hear him say, "Hello your majesty. Mhmm, mhmm. Of course, come in!"

What?

James comes back in with his hands out in front of him, cupped around something- or someone.

"Sis, Acari is here so you can tell her everything that happened!"

"Yes," Ateil says, sitting up beside me. "Tell us everything."

So for the second time that day, I recall the story of everything that happened, from Obsidian being my first guest in two years to me stopping Zara with the Frost Flower.

When I am done, they have the same single-word, single-syllable response that I received from everyone else: "Wow."

"Seriously? I tell you how Obsidian, Xara, and I basically just saved the world and the only response I get from all of you is one, single syllable word? Wow."

This gets everyone to laugh.

"What else could we say?" Islana asks.

"Wait, did you say that you created a hurricane and got it to pinpoint down on one target?" Ateil asks.

"Yes," I confirm.

"Wow. You may need to be a master and I'll be the apprentice!"

I smile. Wait, didn't Mama say that the academy might open up again?

"Is the academy going to open again soon?"

"Maybe. It all depends," Mama says.

I frown. "Depends on what? On if we can rebuild it?"

"No. It depends on whether we can return the light to the Sun on time."

"How long do we have before the Sun goes out forever?"

"About three days at the most," Xara responds.

Three days? Can't we catch a break?

As if reading my thoughts, Papa says, "Let the council handle this one. You kids should take a break. Ateil, you will need to report to the council to help them."

Take a break? Scratch what I said earlier. How exactly do they expect us to "take a break"?! But when I take a look at his face, I know that there is no changing his mind.

When Papa isn't looking, Ateil bumps my arm and whispers into my ear, "Don't worry. I have no intention of letting you miss out on this."

I smile. I missed Ateil so much.

Chapter Twenty-Eight: Get Some Actual Sleep!

Perhaps Islana heard Ateil say this, or perhaps it was sheer luck, but she chose that moment to say, "Why don't we let you seven talk more about your adventures? Come on Aya and Telek, Kirana and Telesto are waiting for us."

Telesto is Obsidian's grandfather.

Wait. *Seven*? Me, Obsidian, Xara, and Ateil make four. Who are the other three? Oh. Wait. She means Acari, James, and Sev. I take a quick glance at their faces and instantly know that there is no way to talk them out of helping. Well, if you can't beat them, join them.

As soon as the adults leave, Ateil says, "Lyra, Obsidian, and Xara, meet me in Lyra's library at midnight. Acari, James, and Sev, you can go at five AM. No way are we leaving you out of this!"

"Wait, what library?" Xara asks. I forgot that this was her first time here. No, wait, she has been here for two days now while I was unconscious. Even so, I shouldn't expect her to know where my library is. Not even my parents know where it is. It can only be accessed from two parts of the house: my room, and Ateil's room.

Masters and professors don't usually live with their apprentice, but it turns out that Ateil is my cousin so she lives with us. I can hear you saying, "What?" out there so I guess I never told you that fact.

"Why don't you two sleep in here tonight?" I suggest. "It would be much easier to show you where to go than to tell you directions."

Obsidian and Xara nod enthusiastically.

"Okay then, it's settled. You all get some sleep now," Ateil commands.

What? "What? I was just unconscious for two days! I don't need sleep!"

"Yes, you do. Look, Jupiter is up now. Time for sleep!"

"But-" I start to argue but Ateil is already gliding towards the door.

"Great, see you three at midnight!" With that, Ateil marches out of my room with Sev and James trailing after her, Acari still in his hands.

I sigh.

Obsidian bumps my arm. "Hey, cheer up. We get to have a slumber party!"

I laugh. "Okay, okay, I guess I should 'cheer up' and 'get some sleep.'"

We all get our pajamas on and brush our teeth, completely skipping dinner. For some strange reason, I am not that hungry anyway.

"Where do we sleep?" Xara asks.

Obsidian grins. "In the hammocks of course!"

Another thing my parents don't know about my room: I have several hammocks in it.

Obsidian moves over to my backup lamp and pushes a button on it, so small you would never notice it unless you knew it was there.

The back wall behind my bed slides over, revealing two hammocks, made out of silk the Water Weavers wove. And by "Water Weavers", I mean Mama.

"Cool!" Xara breathes.

Obsidian laughs at her reaction as he climbs into his hammock.

"Aren't you going to bed Lyra?" he asks.

"One moment!" I call. I grab the earring chain that held Ateil's Homaso and toss it out my always-open window. I peer out in time to see Eloh gobble it up.

Satisfied, I slide under my cool covers and fall asleep with my house full again for the first time in two years. And for the first time in three days, I sleep at the right time, in the right place, and actually have a spark of hope that everything will be alright.

Epilogue

I yawn and toss a book down.

"Getting tired already?" Obsidian teases.

I smack him with a book. We had arrived an hour earlier to find Ateil in my library, adding books to an already huge pile. "Read these!" she had said.

"No, I just wish we could find some answers."

I had already read the 500-page book *Secrets Of The Sun* and am now reading the book *A Guide To Healing Our Solar System.*

"Are you sure that we will find something in these books?" I ask.

Ateil nods, not looking up from her book.

As if the books heard my plea, a book falls from the pile in front of me. Right to a page on the solid drop of light that fuels the Sun.

I pick it up and gasp. This page tells you how to replace it!

"I found it!" I announce, not worrying about my family hearing me. We are deep underground.

Everyone quickly gathers around me and Ateil gently snatches the book from me. She scans it and smiles.

"Well?" Obsidian asks. "What does it say?"

"Do you want the good news or the bad news first?" she asks.

Well, that's easy. "The bad news of course!" I say. My friends nod.

"Well, we need to get supplies from the Human world. Also, we can't do this from Earth so after we visit the Human world, we need to go to Mercury. We all can stay with our cousins there."

I'm sorry, did I hear that right? I don't think that my ears are working properly.

Obsidian must be thinking the same thing because he asks, "We have cousins on Mercury?!"

"Yes, that is what I said."

Me and Obsidian look at each other, bewildered. Only Xara doesn't seem surprised by that bit of information.

"We have to go to the Human's world?" Obsidian practically has steam coming out of his ears. I touch his arm to calm him down. I know how he feels about Humans ever since his parents went missing in their world. Sometimes I feel the same way about them.

"And the good news?" Xara asks weakly, trying to calm down the situation.

"The good news is that this has been done before. And with *each* of your abilities, you will be able to get the job done."

Something about the way she says that makes me think back and realize that I have never seen Xara's ability.

"Hey Xara, what is your ability? Why didn't you use it against your sister?"

She looks away and mutters something unintelligible that I think is, "It couldn't have helped."

I narrow my eyes at her. First, she wasn't exactly open about her family, now she won't tell us what her ability is. What is she hiding? Is she a Water Weaver? A Camishift? Or maybe a...

"We leave tomorrow morning at five-thirty AM," Ateil announces, interrupting my thoughts.

"Five thirty AM?!" we all cry.

She rolls her eyes. "Yes. Now go get some sleep! I expect you to be here at five AM, ready for the day!"

With that order, she marches away to either her bedroom or the kitchen, I don't know which.

"Well," Obsidian starts, breaking the silence. "Better make these next four hours of sleep count!"

Amaranth is very tired and cold. And cranky. She had failed herself- she means her "master". She helped her "master" escape Eloh but she decided not to escape. She had known that Zara would be back and she had been correct.

Oh, why does she risk everything for her "master"?

Because she will help me rule the galaxy! she reminds herself. She shivers and wraps her jacket tightly around her. She is very cold.

Wait. Cold. That means that she must be getting close to her master!

"Hang on! I am coming 'master'!" she calls into the darkness, sarcasm dripping off her tongue on the word "master".

She runs and trips on something.

Grumbling, she sits back up and blindly looks around for what she tripped over. Finally, her hands find a broken earring chain. Could it be? No, it couldn't. Amaranth is almost too afraid to look but she must.

Lightning bolts. It is the earring! She can't tell which one it is in the darkness, so she holds it up to the moonlight and sees that the gems have turned black.

Amaranth gasps as she realizes what this means. That silly girl freed her! And stole what was unrightfully hers! Now what was she going to do?

Go into hiding? No. No one knows that this was her real identity. Everyone thought that she was Camo. She is safe. *Is she though?*

She must take back what was stolen from her before that prisoner or bothersome girl frees it again.

She grabs the earring and flees back into the darkness, all thoughts of freeing her "master" blown out of her mind by just the thought of the broken earring.

She will free her "master" once it is safe to do so. Once she has the leverage to take her master over.

Then, and only then will she be "forgiven" and finally have the power she has sacrificed so much for.

First, however, she needs to get out of here. And she knows just how to do it.

Willow Academy Overview

Willow Weather Sorceresses School:

Weather Sorceress Overview:

- Weather sorceresses can control the weather based on their will or very strong emotions. The most powerful of the weather sorceresses can create giant storms like hurricanes.

What You Learn At Willow:

- At Willow, we will teach you how to control the weather so it does not get taken over by strong emotions like grief, great joy, or love. The most powerful of you will learn how to conjure hailstorms, short tornadoes, and hurricanes.

Willow Camishift School:

Camishift Overview:

- Camishifts can look like anyone or anything. They are most often named after a gem. People had such a hard time finding their kids that they started infusing them with a mineral or gem and naming them after it. Then, if you need to find them, you just squeeze the gem that is their namesake and they have no choice but to appear. Only the most responsible Camishifts are not named after a stone. Once a Camishift is deemed responsible, their stone is extracted from them and they get a new name. Very few Camishifts have the gift of complete freedom.

What You Learn At Willow:

- We will teach you how to transform into the most difficult of things like animals and people. The most skilled of you will learn how to shift into something by description only. At the end of graduation, we have been given the right to deem Camishifts responsible and therefore the right to extract stones.

Willow Telepath School:

Telepath Overview:

- Telepaths can hear thoughts and block them as well. They can also hear emotions and pictures that people see in their mind. A telepath may read someone's mind without permission as long as they get permission if they are going to share that person's thoughts. Telepaths can also use their ability to communicate with others.

What You Learn At Willow:

- At Willow, we will teach you how to block thoughts so you don't get headaches. We will also teach you how to use your ability to communicate telepathically with someone as well. The most skilled of you will go on missions to court to see if someone is telling the truth.

Water Weaver School:

Water Weaver Overview:

- Water Weavers can weave water into silk that can be turned into dresses, hammocks, and beds. They can make water appear in the desert, make jugs that automatically refill with water, control oceans, and create rivers.

What You Learn At Willow:

- At Willow, you will start by learning how to weave water into silk and go from there. If you are dedicated and go through four Sun rotations of training, you will learn how to control oceans. The more skilled of you will learn how to make jugs that automatically refill with water.

Gravitational Wizard School:

Gravitational Wizard Overview:

- What gravitational wizards do is similar to what you Humans call telekinesis. They can bend gravity so they can climb on walls, stop them or other people from falling, or to make up down and down up.

What You Learn At Willow:

- At Willow, we will teach you how to bend gravity to your will so you or someone else can float. As your concentration grows, you will be able to expand your release on gravity and we will be able to use it to bring objects to you.

Note: Some abilities are not taught at Willow because they are simply too rare. Only one person every century will have one of these abilities. Only one person has ever been known to have two rare abilities. For example: Plantspeak, Timetrapers, and Infusers will not be able to learn their abilities at Willow. Our sincerest apologies. However, anyone spotted with a rare ability will immediately be admitted into the council.

Character Guide In Case You Forgot Who Is Who:

(Note: People from the Hidden Forest do not tend to have last names.)

- ❖ Acari:

> Age: Unknown

> Ability: None

> Who They Are: The worm queen

- ❖ Ateil:

> Age: 21

> Ability: Weather Sorceress

> Who They Are: Lyra's cousin and her master/professor

- ❖ Aya:

> Age: Unknown

> Ability: Water Weaver

> Who They Are: James and Lyra's mother

❖ Camo:

> Age: Unknown

> Ability: Camishift

> Who They Are: Zara's "assistant." Real name unknown (unless you read the epilogue)

❖ Islana:

> Age: Unknown

> Ability: Plantspeak and Infuser

> Who They Are: Lyra and James's Tia and professor

❖ James:

> Age: Nine

> Ability: Camishift

> Who They Are: Lyra's brother

❖ Kirana:

> Age: Unknown

> Ability: Weather Sorceress

> Who They Are: Obsidian's grandmother

❖ Lyra:

> Age: 11

> Ability: Weather Sorceress, Telepath

> Who They Are: James' sister and Obsidian's best friend

❖ Obsidian:

> Age: 11

> Ability: Camishift and Telepath

> Who They Are: Lyra's best friend

❖ Sev:

> Age: Eight (Magic People age) and fifty (actual age)

> Ability: None

> Who They Are: Tree spirit that Lyra freed

❖ Telek:

> Age: Unknown

> Ability: Gravitational Wizard

> Who They Are: Lyra and James's father

❖ Telesto:

> Age: Unknown

> Ability: Timetrapper

> Who They Are: Obsidian's grandfather

❖ Xara:

> Age: 19

> Ability: Unknown

> Who They Are: Lyra's other best friend and twin sister of the evil Zara

❖ Zara/Araz:

> Age: 19

> Ability: Weather Sorceress

> Who They Are: Xara's evil twin

Words You Should Know By Now But Here They Are With Their Definitions In Case You Forgot:

- **Camishift**: A person who can look like anyone or anything. What you Humans simply call a shapeshifter.
- **Magic People**: People who can harness the "magic" of Nature.
- **Homaso**: Stands for "Holder Of Magic And Spirit Orb".
- **Spiritine Crystal**: A special crystal that connects with one's spirit and soul to free them.
- **Ttufos Machine**: Stands for Transportation Through the Universal Fabric Of Space. So simply what you Humans call a teleporting machine.

Don't miss out!

Visit the website below and you can sign up to receive emails whenever Pila Chapman publishes a new book. There's no charge and no obligation.

https://books2read.com/r/B-A-ZZPMC-YXCBF

BOOKS 2 READ

Connecting independent readers to independent writers.

About the Author

Hi!

I'm Pila!

I love to read books, learn science, and invent things.

I live in a beautiful forest with my family.

Thanks to everyone who read this!

(More books coming soon!)